WO
APART

GAIL VINALL

Scripture Union
130 City Road, London EC1V 2NJ.

By the same author:
Walking Disaster – Impressions

The Project – Tiger Book
A Family for Ben – Tiger Book
Roughshod Ride – Leopard Book

© Gail Vinall 1992
First published 1992

ISBN 0 86201 754 8

British Library Cataloguing-in-Publication Data.
A catalogue record for this book is available from the British
Library.

Phototypeset by Intype, London
Printed and bound in Great Britain by Cox and Wyman Ltd,
Reading.

~1~

Caro McCarthy sat on the wall which surrounded the school fish pond swinging her legs to the rhythm of the music throbbing from her Walkman. She kept a lookout for her friend who should be appearing through the school gate any moment. Lucy was always late. She simply couldn't organise herself. Caro, on the other hand, was prepared for almost any emergency. Her class-mates had realised early in the first year that if you needed a spare pen, tissue, money for the phonebox, or even an Elastoplast, Caro could usually oblige. Not that you would dare ask twice, however. Caro accepted the fail-ings of other people but she was not prepared to be used. Beneath the composed exterior there was quite a temper if provoked.

Caro frowned in the direction of the main gates, her clear blue eyes boring into Lucy who was trotting, red-faced, up the drive.

'Sorry! I had to . . .'

'Come on, we'll be late for Careers,' Caro interrupted, snapping her Walkman off and jumping lightly down from the wall.

'Hang on, I'm out of breath!' Lucy panted, running a hand through the brown curls which clung to her damp forehead.

'It's not my fault if you can't get up on time,' Caro called over her shoulder.

Lucy grinned. She knew how annoyed Caro became with her lack of punctuality, but neither girl would change and they would always be best friends, despite their differences.

'What's so interesting about Careers anyway?' Lucy shouted.

'Honestly, Lucy, you can't have forgotten! We find out today about our work experience placements.'

'Oh that!'

'*Lucy*, this could be crucial to our future careers.'

'When I leave school, I'm going to get married and have hundreds of babies.'

Caro spun round and opened her mouth to protest but Lucy's elfish smile stopped her. 'I know you're just winding me up, Lucy Baker.'

'Well, I certainly don't want some high-powered office job where you're all burnt out by the time you're forty. Life isn't all work, you know.'

'Life isn't much work at *all* where you're concerned,' Caro laughed, tucking her hand under Lucy's elbow in an attempt to hurry her along.

'At least I have time to relax and be myself. I'd be happy working as a nanny or in an old people's home, cheering them all up.'

'It's not very good pay,' Caro remarked, though feeling guilty at how mercenary she sounded.

'I just hope you'll be able to enjoy all the money you make when you take over the stock market!' Lucy returned.

'Financial management doesn't mean the stock market necessarily. I like organising people . . .'

'Bossing them around, you mean!'

'Well, I don't manage with *you*, do I?' Caro said, darting inside the Careers classroom just in time to prevent Mrs Clarke from closing the door on them.

'Ah, the last two. Good. Now sit down everyone and pay attention.'

Caro slid her notebook and pencil onto the desk quickly, while beside her Lucy rummaged noisily in the bottom of a bag for a much-chewed biro. Mrs Clarke paused until everyone was concentrating before she shook three typed pages out of a buff envelope and began to read out some lists. After each name and tutor group came the name of some firm or organisation to which the pupil was allotted. Caro tensed with excitement. She had put her name down for management experience with either a bank or large retail outlet.

'Lucy Baker, form 4A, Fountain Nursery for pre-school children.'

'Oh great!' Lucy cooed, shooting forward in her chair.

'They start at 8.30 am, Lucy. I trust that won't be a problem?' Mrs Clarke said, to the amusement of the rest of the class.

'I won't be late for *that*, Miss,' Lucy protested.

Caro grinned at her friend, glad that she had got what she wanted. Crawling around with dozens of under-fives was not her idea of a useful work placement but Lucy would love every minute. Now to await her own fate. The names in alphabetical order slid by, usually accompanied by a groan or a happy sigh depending on whether the placement was expected or not. When Caro finally heard her name announced, she flipped her note-pad over, pencil hovering above in anticipation.

'Caro McCarthy, form 4A, Michael's Hair Stylists, mornings only. Afternoons at The Cats' Protection League, Sidley Road.'

'Gosh!' Lucy said, glancing at Caro's face but there was no visible reaction. Only the slightly shaking fingers holding the pencil betrayed Caro's feelings. There was worse to come.

'Simon Mitchel, you'll be with Caro at Michael's Hair Stylists, and I'd like to think you can make a better impression than you did at Cowleys Garage last month.'

Simon Mitchel, the drop-out of form 4C, unwrapped his long legs and spread them into the aisle between the rows of desks. He shifted in his seat and muttered something inaudible. Caro stole a glance at him and felt her lip curl. She did not like Simon. From his long dark hair to his scruffy trainers he was one pack of trouble. Never overtly rude to teachers, he still managed to oppress every lesson with his insolent expression and utter boredom with school. Even Caro thought that Mrs Clarke's placement was ridiculous. She couldn't imagine them letting him through the door looking like that. He didn't exactly smell but his skin looked grubby, his collar was never ironed and that hair! Had it ever seen a comb? It was bad enough having to go to a hairdresser's at all let alone with that hunk of uselessness.

Outside the classroom, Lucy tried to console Caro. 'I suppose it's sort of management, after all Michael's only opened last year and it's the most trendy place in town now. That's enterprise for you.'

'But I don't *want* to be a hairdresser for goodness sake, and the owner *is* the manager. He's hardly going to spend time letting me learn book-keeping or ordering. I'll be sweeping up and making the coffee. What a waste of time!'

'Well, there's always the cats' home,' Lucy said timidly.

'The cats' home! What was Mrs Clarke thinking of? Susie Jenkins wants to be a vet – she's ended up at Debenhams! The woman's off her rocker.'

'Well, I wouldn't mind working with those animals.'

'Oh yeah, *more* sweeping up and coffee making. I might even get to open the tins of Whiskas.'

Lucy fell silent. Caro was determined to be in a mood so there was no point in trying to cheer her up. As far as Lucy was concerned, two weeks off school was brilliant *whatever* you were doing. Caro took everything far too seriously.

'Are you going in to lunch?'

'I suppose so.' Caro took a deep breath and slung her bag over her shoulder. They joined the queue straggling from the canteen door down the steps to the science labs.

'I wish 4th years were allowed an early lunch like the

5ths,' Lucy moaned as they edged slowly forward.

'Ow, watch it!' Caro shouted, as the girl in front stepped back onto her toes.

'It's that yob! He pushed in,' the girl exclaimed.

'Who is it?' Lucy asked, peering over Caro's shoulder.

'Who else?'

Ahead of them, Simon Mitchel was elbowing into position at the head of the queue, oblivious to the threats of the dinner lady who was attempting in vain to keep order.

'Go to the back, Simon Mitchel!'

'Get lost!' he returned, enjoying her shocked expression.

'He'd never dare say that to a teacher!' Caro said. 'I really hate that boy. He's so mouthy and such a slob.'

'He's got a pretty rough home life, they say,' Lucy replied mildly.

'*Who* says?' Caro demanded.

'Oh, you know, it gets around. His mum left last year and his dad's never home.'

'I'd leave home if I had a son like that,' Caro returned.

'I know. Still, it can't be easy.'

'It's no excuse for being downright rude. Oh good, Mr Webber's here. He'll sort him out,' Caro observed with satisfaction.

'Mitchel!' The deputy head's voice resounded down the corridor. Moments later, Mitchel loped, hands stuffed into pockets, to the back of the queue. As he passed them he glared at Caro, catching sight of her cool smile. His dark eyes smouldered dangerously and Caro took an involuntary step back. The boy showed his teeth which were surprisingly white. He grinned like a dog – it could have been friendly or a warning. With a furtive glance he stepped into the queue behind Lucy.

'What do you think you're doing?' Caro demanded, two red spots of colour growing in each cheek.

'What's it look like? Anyway, what's it to you? I'm not in front of you,' he snarled.

'You've still pushed in!' Caro flamed.

'Oh, it's Miss Goody Two-Shoes. Superwoman to the rescue,' he mocked.

Lucy giggled nervously.

'If you don't get out right now . . .'

'You'll what?' Simon said, looming over her.

Caro refused to be intimidated. 'I'll get Mr Webber.'

'Running to teacher!'

'Just because you're an ugly great oaf, you don't frighten me,' Caro said, tossing her long blonde hair indignantly.

Anger burned in Simon's eyes. 'Stuck-up cow,' he muttered before he strode away, banging through the outer doors leading into the playground.

'There, that's the way to deal with bullying cowards!' Caro announced, exhilarated by her small victory.

'I'm not sure that was very clever,' Lucy remarked.

'What do you mean?'

'Well, you've got to work with him next week. It could be a bit difficult.'

'I bet he'll mitch off after the first morning. He's just a loser,' Caro decided, turning her attention to the menu board displayed outside the canteen.

Caro didn't spare another thought for Simon Mitchel until a chance meeting later that week outside the church she attended with her parents. This was a special meeting on a Thursday evening in aid of the Urban Fund – a charity set up to help deprived youngsters in inner city areas. Caro didn't live in an inner city area, in fact Wethinbourne was a moderate sized town in what was considered to be a fairly well-off area. The film pictures of sordid tower blocks and run-down shopping centres had been a shock. Following the talk, the main fund-raising part of the evening had been an auction of antiques and knitwear. It seemed more an auction of jumble to Caro's untrained eye, but her mum was clutching a wall plate which she had bid over £5 for, and her dad sported a new Aran sweater knitted by the WI craft section.

'It's a bit itchy!' Mr McCarthy said, tugging at the neck.

'It'll soften up when I wash it,' his wife promised.

'Did you buy anything, Caro?' her dad asked.

'These!' Caro held up a string of imitation pearls and a cheap but pretty brooch. They were quite valueless as antiques but well worth the £2 she had bid for them.

'Hm, I suppose you're all spent out then?'

'Why?'

'I was hoping you'd treat us to fish and chips.'

'Graham, you *can't* be hungry again!' Mrs McCarthy exclaimed.

'Well, *I* am,' Caro said. 'We only had a salad for tea.'

'Oh all right. Here Caro, nip in and get them while we fetch the car.' Mrs McCarthy fished in her bag for her soft, well-worn purse and handed it over.

Across the road from the church the chippie sign glowed warmly and a smell of oil and batter drifted out onto the pavement. Luckily there were only a few people in front of Caro. She stood eyeing the last golden pieces of fish, hoping no one would buy them before her turn. It was some minutes before Caro recognised the figure lounging against the counter, although that long dark hair and the jeans jacket were pretty distinctive. Simon Mitchel was chatting to the shop owner as if they knew each other well. Caro didn't mean to overhear their conversation but the stout fish frier had a rich booming voice, difficult to ignore.

'Here you are, get your stomach around that.'

'Ta, Jack.' Simon tucked a great package of chips under his arm. He didn't seem to care about the grease stain already appearing through the white paper. He lingered chatting, while Jack served the next customer.

'Where's your dad, tonight?'

'Out. Down the pub I guess.'

Jack sniffed disapprovingly.

Simon was searching in his pocket for some coins. 'Can I have a couple of pickled onions, Jack?'

'Here, help yourself, lad. Put your money away.'

9

Simon smiled – a really wide happy smile, Caro noticed. Just like a kid who's been given a present.

'See you tomorrow, Jack.'

'Look after yourself, lad.'

Simon slouched out, only catching sight of Caro at the last moment. He kind of froze and the happy smile faded. That horrible snarl returned, and Caro knew in an instant that he hated her just as much as she disliked him. It made her feel uncomfortable, here, on what was definitely his territory. 'See you tomorrow,' he'd said. Did he eat here *every* night? Why didn't his dad cook, or was he at the pub every night? Caro felt a niggle of guilt at the things she'd said about Simon. Talking to Jack he had sounded really nice and rather vulnerable.

As Caro ordered her food, Jack's face showed nothing. He was quietly polite, disinterested. Caro paid her money thoughtfully and nearly started walking in the wrong direction up the road until Mr McCarthy sounded the horn.

'Where were you off to?' he laughed, as Caro eased into the back seat.

'I got distracted. See that boy?'

'The tall one?'

'Yes. He's in my class. He's doing his work experience with me at Michael's.'

'Perhaps they'll give him a free haircut,' Mrs McCarthy said.

'I shouldn't think he'll last long enough.'

'Why?'

'Oh, he's useless. Always missing school and being rude to the teachers.'

'Why a hairdresser then?'

'I think it's Mrs Clarke's way of getting her own back. He walked out of his last placement after telling the boss where to go.'

'Caro!'

'Well, he did. I hate him,' Caro added viciously.

'That's a bit strong, isn't it? I've never even heard you mention him before.'

'He's a dead loss, that's why.'

'He must have *some* redeeming feature,' Caro's mum said, twisting round in the seat to look at her daughter.

'None that I know of.'

'Well you never ought to judge people before you get to know them.'

'Who'd want to get to know him!'

'Oh dear! Sounds like he's really rattled your cage,' Mr McCarthy grinned turning the car into their drive.

'He called me a stuck-up cow actually,' Caro said, as they piled out of the car. The memory still hurt. She wasn't sure why. It wasn't as if anything Simon Mitchel said could possibly worry her.

'And what did you call him?' her dad said, shooting chips onto warmed plates as his wife put ketchup and pickles onto the kitchen table.

Caro, licking her fingers, glanced at her dad in surprise. He didn't miss much. Maybe 'ugly oaf' had stuck in Simon's mind too. Maybe that explained his hateful expression tonight.

'I think you ought to try and help this boy make a go of next week's placement,' Mr McCarthy said. He flung the sweater off and rolled up his shirt sleeves. The strong arms were hairy. Mr McCarthy was a partner in his own company now, but he could never shake off his preference for the manual side. The grease stains over each knuckle betrayed his visit to the workshop earlier that day. Paperwork was a necessary evil – he was much happier under the bonnet of a car. Caro always described her dad as a company director, which he *was*. Mr McCarthy embarrassed her sometimes by telling people he was a mechanic. That was also true, but it didn't have the same ring. Did that make Caro stuck-up, a snob? She chewed her chips absent-mindedly, lost in thought.

Mrs McCarthy tied an apron around her plump waist and started to wash up, one eye on a pan of warming milk. The kitchen was cosy, bright and clean. It was Caro's favourite room in the whole house. She tried to imagine her mum gone and her dad, who barely ever went out alone, down at the pub. She couldn't. Simon Mitchel's life was about a billion light years away from her own. They had nothing in common at all. Just as she had no real contact with the deprived youngsters of the inner cities.

'Do you think there's any point in giving money to good causes?' Caro asked, accepting the mug of hot chocolate her mum had passed.

'Of course!' Mrs McCarthy pronounced warmly. She was always so confident about her opinions.

'But a few photos can't possibly tell you anything. Wouldn't it be better to go and *see* for yourself?' Caro persisted.

'It depends *why* you want to see,' Mr McCarthy said. He flipped through the evening paper as he talked. 'I can see pictures of famine and disaster almost every week. Seeing doesn't do anything for these poor souls.'

'But you could get first-hand experience of their life – really understand their problems.'

'Some people have to go. They have talents they can use on the spot. But for most of us, going along for a gawk is just grotesque curiosity. I believe those pictures, I trust the word of that speaker tonight, but I can't drop everything and go. What I *can* do is donate some money and use my business influence to sponsor some kid on a training scheme maybe.'

'One kid, but there were hundreds of unemployed kids in those slides tonight, and there are thousands of starving people in the world.'

'Would you like to just ignore them then?'

'No, of course not, but a few pounds here and there seems . . .'

'A drop in the ocean?' her dad suggested.

'Yes, exactly.'

'Well, that may be true but remember what Jesus said. If you give some thirsty traveller a glass of water, it's as if you were giving a drink to him. Every penny or every prayer for someone in need is worthwhile in God's eyes. If you can manage more, all well and good; if not, you've done your best.'

'In any case,' Mrs McCarthy added, 'if everyone gives a little it all adds up and things can really be done to improve conditions.'

'Take that lad you pointed out,' Mr McCarthy began, warming to his theme. 'As far as you're concerned, he's a lost cause, a no-hoper.'

'Simon Mitchel isn't exactly a charitable case,' Caro argued. 'He's only got himself to blame for his problems . . .' She trailed off remembering the kind of home Simon came from. 'Well, some of them anyway,' Caro conceded.

'It's still in your power to give him a helping hand.'

'How?'

'Next week of course. Talk to him, help him get on with the work. It's not the easiest thing – a big lad like him getting stuck in a hairdressers.'

'Or for me!' Caro said. 'It wasn't exactly my first choice either if you remember.'

'Yes, but you're a girl.'

'It's a unisex shop, Dad, and anyway stop being so sexist!'

'Actually the top hair stylists are generally men,' Mrs McCarthy reminded them.

Caro fingered her new brooch reflectively. Had she really made a difference to some inner city child because of this insignificant purchase? If so, she would never see the results. You could only trust that the money would get to the right place. Being just a little nicer to Simon Mitchel would be a lot more costly in terms of her pride, but maybe the effort would be worth it. If he managed to complete a week's placement he'd at least get a decent reference from Mrs Clarke. It might make him less difficult in Careers lessons, might give him a reason to smile just occasionally at school.

Monday morning at 9.00am saw Caro arriving at Michael's Salon in her smartest casual wear and a pair of flat sandals. Her mum had warned about the perils of being on your feet all day in high heels. Taking a deep breath, Caro yanked the heavy door open and entered the reception area. The distinctive smell of perm lotion and shampoo met her nostrils. A young girl only just out of school glanced up from an enormous wicker fan-backed chair and smiled. She was heavily made up and wore a lot of large, flashy bangles.

'You must be the work-experience girl. Have a seat and I'll get Michael.'

'Thank you.'

Caro sank into a sumptuous armchair which was very soft and enveloping. There was a long wait while early clients were deposited momentarily in armchairs before being divested of their coats, swathed in lemon-coloured robes and whisked behind a bead curtain to the inner recesses of the shop. The stylists who appeared to collect their clients occasionally glanced at Caro and she was afraid of being hustled away and shampooed with all the others. Somewhere a coffee percolator blurped and the delicious smell of fresh coffee mixed with the shampoo perfume, making the air heady and fragrant. Still Michael did not appear. Caro checked her watch – 9.30. So much for punctuality.

A cool breeze whipped around her legs as the door opened. Caro glanced up, expecting to see another tousle-haired client, but instead met Simon's dark-ringed eyes. He grunted an acknowledgement and slumped down beside her. Caro edged her skirt in, away from the filthy jeans.

'Bit late, aren't you?' The words were out before Caro could bite them back.

'Been rushed off your feet then?' he asked sarcastically.

'We were told to report at 9.00 am.'

'Doesn't look as if anyone told *Michael*, does it?' Simon pronounced the name with an ill-concealed sneer. 'I suppose he's still poncing around with his rollers in.'

Caro felt the usual wave of disgust beginning. Simon was so crude and insensitive. Controlling her temper with difficulty, Caro attempted polite conversation.

'Had a good weekend?'

Simon glared suspiciously, 'What's it to you?'

'I only *asked.*'

'It was OK.'

There was an awkward pause during which time two more clients arrived. There was nowhere for them to sit and Caro started to get to her feet but Simon made no move.

'Sit down – they're going in anyway,' he grunted, and Caro sat down again, smiling apologetically at the women to cover her embarrassment.

'What did you do then?' Simon began.

'When?'

'Over the weekend.'

'Oh.' Caro steered her brain back to its original tack. 'I went shopping on Saturday, saw a film in the afternoon. Went to church with my parents on Sunday.'

'Huh!'

It was hard to tell whether the 'Huh' was sarcastic or disinterested. Caro fell silent. Simon picked at a stone in the sole of his trainers with dirty nails. Shampooing might be a good job for him, Caro thought.

'Ah, you're here. Sorry to keep you waiting.'

Caro struggled out of the plush cushions with difficulty and put out her hand which Michael shook firmly. Simon, she noticed, kept his hands firmly in his pockets, but he seemed to be changing his ideas about what Michael would be like. The man was tall, fortyish, with very short black straight hair and a well-tanned complexion. His sharp penetrating eyes took them both in at a glance, but his expression gave nothing away. He was dressed casually but expensively. It was all designer labels yet well-worn. He smelled very fresh and clean.

'Come on through. We'll find you overalls, then I'll tell you a bit about our set-up before you begin work. Coffee, sugar?'

They found themselves rapidly and efficiently organised without feeling rushed or embarrassed. It was a clever management knack, Caro thought, and made a mental note to follow Michael's example carefully. Simon was belligerent to the point of rudeness and Caro found herself being ultra-polite to compensate.

'We'll get you both on shampooing this morning. It's a basic skill but it's where our clients begin, so our service has to be spot on. Watch Sandra.'

They stood unobtrusively around the apprentice and followed the shampoo, rinse, conditioner, rinse procedure. Sandra's fingers moved firmly yet sensitively and not a drop of water came within three inches of the client's face. She made frequent checks about the water temperature or the angle of the sloping chair, yet still managed to maintain an easy conversation. Thick warm towels were used liberally and then discarded into a huge wash basket nearby. At the end of the operation, which had taken barely five minutes, the client was guided to the stylist's chair looking relaxed and smiling.

'Easy, isn't it!' Michael said. 'The stylist will guide you as to which shampoo to use, but as a rough guide normal hair needs the cream lotion, greasy the green herbal, and dry or permed the lanolin extract. Think you can remember that?'

Caro nodded, her head spinning.

'Your first two clients are arriving. I'll introduce you.'

For the next hour Caro was busy, shampooing, percolating coffee and emptying the wash basket. Three tumble driers hummed constantly in a backroom as they were fed piles of damp towels to be regurgitated fluffy and dry after thirty minutes. Caro found herself enjoying things. At any rate the time flew by. She was vaguely aware of Simon working beside her, but was too busy chatting politely or concentrating on the fierce jet of water to pay him much attention. One thing she *was* aware of was his stolid silence and complete refusal to engage anyone in anything other than strictly essential conversation.

At lunch time, Caro promised herself, she would make an effort to be friendly, but when one o'clock arrived Simon whipped off his overalls and was gone.

~2~

When Caro arrived at the salon the following morning she was surprised to see Simon already there. He was sweeping the glossy tiled floor listlessly and didn't bother to look up as Caro passed. Elaine, the head stylist, smiled as Caro shrugged into her overall in the tiny cloakroom.

'Nice to see a smiling face,' Elaine remarked. 'What's up with your friend? Can't get a word out of him this morning.'

'He's not my friend,' Caro said quickly and then felt immediately ashamed. 'I think things are a bit rough at home,' she added. 'He's always pretty quiet.'

'He'll have to buck his ideas up. Michael wasn't impressed with his attitude yesterday afternoon.'

'What happened?' Caro gave in to her curiosity. The previous day she had left early to clock in at the Cats' Protection League. She had only caught a glimpse of Simon returning from a very extended lunch time.

'Oh, he's so surly. Quite rude actually. He refuses to talk to the customers and he left the basins in an awful mess. We can't have someone like that around. I thought St Luke's was a decent school.'

'It *is*!' Caro interrupted hotly. 'Simon just didn't want to do hairdressing, that's all.'

'Why did he agree to come then?'

Caro considered trying to explain about Simon's past record, but decided against it. It wasn't likely to help.

'I expect he'll be OK today now he's settled in,' Caro suggested doubtfully.

'Perhaps you'd better have a word with him then. Michael says you're worth two of Simon any day, even though you're just part-time.'

Caro smiled briefly. The compliment wasn't worth much when you looked at Simon, wielding his broom with that awful scowl darkening his features. He looked as if the slightest irritation could provoke him into smacking it firmly round the next client's shins.

'How's it going?' Caro asked casually as she tidied bottles of mousse and setting gel on the shelves close to where Simon was working.

He grunted inaudibly.

'You could make an effort,' Caro hissed.

'Go, jump!' Simon spat back.

'Look, it's not just *you*. I'm here as well and the school name is on the line. If you get kicked out I'm going to get tarred with the same brush!'

'Has anyone ever told you what an interfering little . . .'

'Hi everyone,' Michael said, appearing from nowhere on moccasin padded feet. 'Plenty to do?'

'Yes, thanks,' Caro said, flushing in case he'd over-heard their exchange.

'You're looking pretty bored with that, lad. Perhaps you'd like to help me with some stocktaking this morning?'

Simon shrugged his shoulders and Caro felt herself squirm. She was sure it was all deliberate.

'I'll finish the sweeping, shall I?' Caro said through gritted teeth, snatching the handle from Simon's slack grasp. He watched her attack the floor for a second and the ghost of a smile flickered around his mouth. Caro ignored him. Why did she have to feel so responsible all the time?

Once the floor was thoroughly swept and every pin,

18

roller, comb and box of tissues arranged precisely, Caro allowed herself a break and a cup of coffee. The routine was busy but at the same time fairly free. The stylists might work all lunchtime, so nobody minded if they were in the kitchen area at odd free moments with their feet up. Caro enjoyed this independence but found it rather off-putting. She was so used to school where you responded like an automaton to bells. After ten minutes she found herself guiltily looking around for jobs. The salon was quiet though, and there was really nothing to do. Caro sighed, bored. She hated to be still. Catching sight of a dishevelled pile of magazines, she pounced on them, discarding the tatty outdated ones and filing the others in a sort of loose classification system. She had just finished when Elaine called her over.

'Mrs Jenkins should be dry by now. Can you check and then take out the rollers, please. If you brush out, I'll be over to style in a minute.'

Pleased but nervous, Caro nodded and turned her attention to the lady under the dryer.

'Would you like to sit over here now?' Caro asked.

The lady continued flicking through her magazine, oblivious to Caro's request. The noise of the dryer had evidently blocked out Caro's voice. Clearing her throat Caro repeated herself, gently touching the lady's shoulder.

'What's that?' Mrs Jenkins boomed.

'I think you're dry now!' Caro trumpetted in her ear.

'No need to shout, dear.'

Acutely embarrassed, Caro watched hesitantly as the old lady collected her handbag, glasses case, stick and handkerchief. Her knees were wide apart in the padded seat and Caro looked away to avoid the acres of floral petticoat and elasticated knickers. As Mrs Jenkins hauled her not insubstantial body out of the seat, she caught her hairnet up in the control button on the edge of the drier.

'Oops, can you sort that out dear?'

With trembling fingers, Caro plucked at the hairnet.

'Ow!' Mrs Jenkins yelled as her thin hair became tangled in the net.

'I'm so sorry,' Caro apologised. What a fiasco, she thought. One or two of the stylists were looking round and grinning. Nobody came to help and Elaine wasn't in sight.

'Can you hurry up, dear, I'm getting a crick in my neck.'

'I'm sorry, Mrs Jenkins, I just can't seem to . . .'

'Here, let me.' From behind her, grubby fingers reached towards the net, deftly twisting the strands until the control knob was freed.

'Oh thanks,' Caro mumbled.

'Let's give you a hand, love,' Simon said, hauling the old lady to her feet. Unaffected by her ungainly wobble, he scooped up her bag and stick and guided her to a nearby chair, practically lifting her off her feet.

'Ooh, you're a strong lad, aren't you?' Mrs Jenkins crowed, her eyes crinkling into laughter lines. 'What's a big lad like you doing here?'

'Who knows!' Simon retorted, flashing her one of his devastating smiles. Caro stood back feeling silly and inadequate.

'Aren't you going to get these pricklers out of my head?' Mrs Jenkins cried.

'Caro'll do that.'

'No, no, you go ahead,' Caro whispered. She felt far too flustered to start unwinding rollers. Instead she stepped back and busied herself arranging Mrs Jenkins' possessions under the work surface before someone fell over them.

Simon was just finishing amid guffaws of laughter from Mrs Jenkins, when Elaine glided up. She took in the scene with a frown.

'Thank you, Simon, I think Michael wants you in the stock cupboard,' she said coolly, brushing him aside. His shoulders immediately sagged and even Mrs Jenkins sobered down. They looked like two naughty school children caught eating sweets in class.

Elaine ignored Caro who was hovering between an

explanation and an apology. In the end she slid away and began collecting up a new batch of damp towels from the wash basket near the sink. Silly woman, she muttered crossly to herself. Simon was managing perfectly. They're determined to find fault with him now.

Ever the defender of the underdog, Caro found herself resenting the way the receptionist sneered whenever Simon passed her and the way Michael kept him out of sight in the dusty rooms behind the salon all morning. He was just being used to hump boxes around while she was being given all the interesting tasks. Perhaps Simon hadn't made much of a start the day before, but Mrs Jenkins had liked him. He'd been great with her, but just because she was deaf and old that didn't count. Caro noticed the way Elaine hustled Mrs Jenkins out of the shop and exchanged a weary look with one of the other stylists when the door finally closed on the ungainly old soul. It wasn't fair. Mrs Jenkins might be deaf and awkward, but she deserved as much attention as the young women who came in to spend hours talking about the latest styles and fingering their way through colour cards when their own hair colour suited them perfectly well. Caro was amazed at how much people were willing to pay just to have the latest image.

She saw one girl with beautiful springy auburn curls have them straightened, not very successfully, and another woman with ordinary but pleasant, straight brown hair spend nearly thirty pounds achieving a frizzled, straggly look. On more than one occasion, she had found herself wanting to say, 'Oh no, that would look awful – I shouldn't bother if I were you!' To be fair, Michael sometimes refused to give people the style they asked for if he thought it wouldn't suit them, but new expensive products were temptingly displayed on the counters and the salon walls were plastered with photographs of exotic styles cut in unusual shapes. Not the sort of thing likely to last well on a damp morning in town. But that was all part of the business. Give someone a style that demanded constant care and they became a regular customer. Mrs Jenkins, who came for a set once a month and a chat, didn't rate very highly in importance, if you wanted to make a profit.

Nevertheless, it was in Caro's nature to give everything to a task and she worked away diligently until Elaine gave her a nod and pointed to her watch. Lunchtime at last. Gratefully, Caro peeled off her overalls, grabbed her shoulder bag and slipped out into the back street. It was another world behind the High Street. Service bays were full of dry leaves and bursting black bags coughed litter into the gutters. Wrinkling her nose, Caro hurried down the back street, emerging into bright sunshine and the bustle of traffic. Lucy was licking tomato juice from her fingers as Caro came up and sprawled beside her on the grass.

'I love this park,' Lucy said, waggling her bare toes. Her shoes were some distance away. 'Had a good morning?'

Caro was noncommittal. She took her sandals off, carefully placed them together a little way from her elbow, then searched in her bag for the neat foil package which contained her lunch. Taking a small bite of cheese sandwich she glanced at her friend.

'I take it you're having a good time?'

'Perfect!' Lucy cooed. She had a dreamy maternal look in her eyes.

'Well, I wish I was with you.'

'Caro, you're joking! All those sticky fingers and dribbly mouths.'

'At least it's useful.'

'So is hairdressing! I don't know where I'd be without someone keeping this lot tamed,' Lucy said, tweaking a curl ruefully.

'Your average hairdressing, yes, but not the sort of thing they do at Michael's.'

'Last night on the phone you thought he was great.'

'I know, but I'm seeing another side of things. It's all just a rip-off.'

'People *choose* to go there. They know the prices.'

'Yes, but they'd look just as good paying half as much – in fact better,' Caro added, remembering frizzle head.

'But that's the art of financial wizardry, isn't it? Give the customer a service they're willing to pay through the nose for?'

'It isn't right.'

'You don't have to tell me! I'm just rehearsing your own arguments. Anyway, how's Simon getting on?'

'Dreadfully!'

'Oh dear, as good as that?'

'It's not funny, Lucy. He'll be given the push soon at the rate he's going.'

'I thought you'd be glad.'

'Of course not!' Caro protested. 'I'm not completely mean. Anyway, the thing is it's not all his fault. Mrs Clarke should never have sent him there. They're just using him as someone to hump boxes around.'

'Perhaps he prefers that.'

'It still isn't fair. They're supposed to give us an insight into all aspects of the job. Just because Simon doesn't look smart they keep him out of sight and don't teach him anything.'

'Maybe he wouldn't be any good.'

'He *is*. He's great with old people, the ones everyone else just takes the mickey out of.'

'Well, what can *you* do? Nothing, so you might as well eat that sandwich instead of picking bits off it, or give it to me.'

Absent-mindedly, Caro took another bite. 'I *will* do something.'

'What?'

'I don't know yet, but they can't go on treating Simon like this.'

'Someone's *really* rattled your cage,' Lucy observed, scattering muesli bar crumbs for a confusion of hungry pigeons head-banging near their feet.

'Maybe I'm not cut out for business after all. It's just not . . .' Caro groped for the right word. 'Christian, I suppose.'

Lucy rolled onto her tummy lazily. 'It isn't "doing to others as you would be done by", you mean?'

'Yes, that's it. It's selling things that people don't really need and that maybe aren't even good for them.'

'A few perms can't hurt.'

'But it's the principle, you see. Who says we have to have hair that curls, or doesn't, or is blonde or black?'

'People want . . .'

'No, they *think* they want, because they've been brainwashed by TV and the media. So they're dissatisfied with what they've got.'

'It's not wrong to want to change.'

'No, so long as it's *you* wanting to change, not some great financial machine persuading you to change for its own profits.'

'A bit heavy for Tuesday lunchtime,' Lucy groaned. 'You sound like Miss Freeman in Social Studies.'

'Well, she's right. We should question the values of society.'

'Hairdressing doesn't sound like a great threat to Christianity to me,' Lucy said.

'Of course it isn't. I'm talking about common business procedures.'

'How was the Cats' Protection League?' Lucy enquired, hoping to change the subject.

'What? Oh fine. It was just a quick visit. I'm there all day Thursday and Friday. Pearl – she's in charge – is a bit eccentric. Wellies and flowery skirts.'

'What about the cats?'

'Didn't see any! I found out some interesting facts though. They neuter every cat they pick up as a stray, and if you own a cat, they'll neuter it free of charge.'

'Poor cats!'

'No, it's great because it means there aren't hundreds of unwanted kittens around. It's really responsible, and if you offer a home to a cat from there, they check up every month for four months to see how things are working out.'

'That's a good idea,' Lucy conceded.

'In fact I'm looking forward to going there a lot more than I'd anticipated.'

'Crikey, Caro, you'll be leaving school to do voluntary work at this rate,' Lucy laughed, as she hauled herself up and shook her skirt.

'It can't be time to go yet!' Caro sighed.

'Afraid so. Must dash. I'll see you at church tonight – Youth Club?'

'Yes. Have a good afternoon.'

'I will,' Lucy laughed smugly.

Caro consulted her watch. Ten to two. Lucy would be early for once in her life. But perhaps it wasn't so very surprising. She was doing something she enjoyed. Work experience certainly *was* a new outlook for them both. If only it could have been for Simon as well. It was just more of the same for him.

When Caro returned to the salon, only a minute early, there was an argument going on in the kitchen between Elaine and Michael. She had no idea about its cause until she was hauled in to listen to a list of complaints about Simon, who was nowhere to be seen.

'Coffee cups not washed up, the floor unswept. Just went off at lunchtime without a word,' Elaine was saying.

'And where is he now? It's your job to allocate lunch-times, not me,' Michael snapped, looking ruffled for once.

'He was with you this morning.'

'I can't have someone like that in the salon . . .'

'Then phone the school and . . .'

Suddenly Caro found herself shaking with rage and indignation. How dare they talk about him when he wasn't even there to defend himself? They were as sweet as could be to *her*, why not Simon?

'Actually, I forgot to wash the cups, I'm sorry,' Caro heard herself say, 'and when you told me to go to lunch, I assumed you meant both of us, so I told Simon we could go. His mum is really ill and he wanted to get back home because she can't get out of bed to fix herself

25

any lunch. The doctor has ordered complete rest, you see, and I expect that's why he's so late back.'

Elaine stared, her lipstick-coated lips apart, before two spots of red began to glow in each cheek. Caro thought she was going to choke as she mumbled, 'Oh well,' and twisted the rings on her hand in embarrassment. Michael looked at Caro steadily with disbelief clearly written in his face. Caro met his stare defiantly and forced herself to keep calm.

'Perhaps you should have told us,' Michael said quietly.

'Simon doesn't like his personal life discussed,' Caro replied, brazening it out. She was appalled at how easily the lies flowed once she got started. It was as if she almost believed it herself.

'Perhaps you could see to these cups now,' Elaine said, 'and in future leave Simon's timetable to me. You *are* only part-time, after all,' she added, before flouncing out of the kitchen.

Caro squirted washing-up liquid gaily and hummed as she scrubbed at congealed sugar crystals in the bottom of cups. Her final grades had just taken a pretty violent hammering, she supposed, but for once in her life she didn't care. Simon was off the hook. Justice had been done and those two might think a bit more carefully about judging people on the way they looked.

There was a moment of panic when Simon rolled in at two-thirty but Caro managed to attract his attention before Elaine pounced.

'Lunchtime was my idea OK, and your sick mother is in bed remember.'

'My *what*?'

'That's why you're late. Don't land me in it after I've covered for you.'

'You?' Simon was completely baffled.

'Ah, Simon, I understand about today, but could we come to a formal arrangement about lunchtime in future? Shall we say an hour and a half from tomorrow. Is that enough?' Elaine suggested.

'Yeah, sure,' Simon grinned.

Caro winked at him encouragingly before returning to the small boy who was refusing to sit still while his hair was combed.

'Well, go on then.'

'What?'

'Why were you late?'

'It's none of your flippin' business!' Simon said, as he swept up for the third time.

'Oh come on, I *did* cover for you after all. I think I have a right to know why.'

'Well, tough because I'm not telling you! And I didn't ask you to lie for me. I thought that was against your principles. Aren't you Christians into honesty? Why lie for *me*?'

'Because I thought they were treating you unfairly, as a matter of fact. I also think you're a fairly nice person, or you could be if you weren't so downright rude and bolshie!' Caro hissed, her former amiable feelings rapidly melting.

'Listen, Miss Two-Shoes. I think this place stinks, and if they'd given me the shove I'd have been glad, so don't think you've done me any favours. You can't earn your Brownie points on me.'

'You ungrateful slob!'

'That's more like it. Now we're back on familiar ground again. The girl I know and love!'

Caro, who knew he was laughing at her, dumped the towels she was holding at his feet and stalked out. How *dare* he, after all she'd done. 'I hope you *do* get sacked,' she called over her shoulder as a parting dig and immediately regretted her childishness.

'You didn't!'

'Yes I did.'

'And then he . . .'

'All right, Lucy, let's not go through it all again. I made a fool of myself, OK. Can we just drop it? Look,

27

Peter is waiting to begin.'

Their minister raised a bushy eyebrow at Lucy who subsided meekly into an armchair. They were both hot from a vigorous game of rounders which had been played on the vicarage lawn. The Strides were not keen gardeners and it gave them, Mrs Stride would laugh, an excuse not to mow the lawn very often if it was the Youth Club cricket-cum-rounders area. Now Peter Stride picked up his Bible and began to read to the two dozen youngsters lounging around him from the passage he had selected earlier that day. Caro listened with half her mind, the other still occupied with the events of the day. Why hadn't Simon been nicer about her sacrifice? Well, it *was* a sacrifice. She'd lied for him and now everything was all mixed up and confusing. Had she been wrong? Had she been 'gathering Brownie points' like he'd said? At the time Caro had just felt sorry for him, but then she'd *wanted* his thanks. That was wrong; so was lying. Even for a good cause? Was it a good cause? Oh, this is useless! Caro concentrated hard on Peter Stride's large hands as they held the Bible. His words filtered through her jumbled thoughts more clearly.

' "And when you do good, do it in secret so that no one will know of your goodness except your father in heaven who sees all things." Remember the widow who had only a small coin to give, but it was valued more highly than the vast sums donated by the rich man. Think *why* God valued her offering more than the larger amount,' Peter asked, gazing at their faces.

'Because it was *everything* she had, so in real terms she gave more?' volunteered Alec who was a statistics whiz.

'Yes, that's partly it.'

'And because she didn't want anyone to see her gift whereas the rich man did,' suggested another quieter boy sitting in the corner.

'Yes, Paul, I think you're right. Jesus said that the rich man had already received his reward. The widow would get her reward in heaven.'

28

Caro remembered with shame her contrary feelings about Simon. She *did* want to help, but she also wanted thanks. Why wasn't it enough just to do the right thing? Perhaps it was something to do with always getting good grades at school. Somehow you came to expect recognition all the time. Simon didn't want to be her charity case, and indeed why should he?

Following the short Bible study, Peter had a few notices to give out about future events, then there was a brief time of prayer. A new spot on the evening agenda was the 'Hot Spot'. Peter had agreed to be grilled on any subject of Christian ethics for ten minutes. The previous week, people had been embarrassed getting started, but this week Caro knew just what she wanted to ask.

The stop watch was set and Peter took the dreaded hot seat. Caro's hand shot up but in fact it was the only one.

'Is it ever right to lie?' she called out.

'Hm, tricky one. As usual, it's one of these "it all depends" issues. Generally speaking, the Bible tells us that our yes should be yes and our no, no, which tells us about the need for loyalty, trust and honest dealings. I can imagine a necessary lie, however. Suppose you are protecting someone from an enemy. The enemy asks where your friend is. I think it might be reasonable to lie or withhold the truth in that case. The vital thing is knowing that your untruthfulness is positively helping you or someone else, not just allowing you or them to escape from responsibilities. Another point to remember of course is that one lie invariably leads to another half dozen. "Oh what a tangled web we weave when first we practise to deceive." Peter loved to quote Shakespeare. 'Does that help at all?'

'Yes, it does, sort of.'

'Well, that's it for tonight, then. Coffee and biscuits before I throw you all out!'

While the others scrambled out of their chairs Caro sat back and relaxed.

'Work experience tiring you out?' Kate Stride asked as

she came to sit beside Caro.

'A bit. It's not like school,' Caro confessed.

'Of course not. The real world never is. Fewer neat corners and straight lines.'

Caro was surprised. The mild and rather mousey woman before her seemed to know exactly how she felt.

'I was interested in your question.'

'Oh that. Something cropped up today at work . . .' There was an air of quiet understanding about Kate. Was it those large grey eyes that invited confidence? Caro wasn't much given to confession. Being a perfectionist, she didn't willingly admit to failures but she found herself pouring out the day's events and Kate proved an intelligent and perceptive listener.

'I put everything on the line for him,' Caro concluded, 'including my honesty, but then he wasn't grateful and yet I don't blame him. I shouldn't have lied for him. There isn't any way I can help him. As a school colleague and as a Christian I just let him down.'

'The Christian label can be a problem in itself sometimes,' Kate said.

'But we're supposed to be proud to say we are!'

'Of course, it's just what some people read into that word that becomes the difficulty. Still, you can't give up.'

'Can't I?' Caro had just been thinking that was the *only* thing to do.

'No. You're probably the only Christian he's ever known. He doesn't *like* you helping him – maybe your motives weren't quite pure – but you've got to prove that however hard he gives you the brush off you won't return it.'

'But I do! I end up abusing him at the end of every conversation!' Caro said in mortification.

'If Simon's had put-downs all his life, which is what it sounds like, you've got to learn not to do what he expects. He may not like it but at least he'll have to take notice. It might make him change his mind about Christians.'

'And I'm supposed to be responsible for *that*?' Caro wailed.

'I thought you enjoyed challenges,' Kate teased.

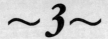

~3~

The Cats' Protection League was housed in a converted bungalow and three enormous sheds which stretched behind it, backing onto enclosed yards which provided exercise areas for the animals. The front lounge of the bungalow was an office-cum-reception area with an adjoining cloakroom. Pearl lived with another helper called Sandy in the rest of the bungalow, sharing with about a dozen cats who were permanent guests. Caro quickly realised why they were not up for adoption. Most were old, irritable, one-eyed, one-eared or had gruesome battle scars. One incredibly agile ginger tom had only three legs. Others had bald patches or eccentric habits which made them useless as potential pets.

'We never put a fit cat down,' Pearl announced proudly, tickling the ginger tom affectionately under the chin.

'So how many cats do you have?' Caro asked.

'At the moment, two hundred and sixty three.'

'It must cost a fortune!' Caro whistled.

'Yes, it does, but we're a registered charity. Local donations are quite good and some people leave us trust funds in their wills. We struggle by. All our food comes in bulk and local suppliers have sponsored us quite well.'

'I've seen your adverts in the paper.'

'Oh yes, that's Sandy. She's quite good at them, but it's difficult thinking up a new catchy line to nudge some prospective cat owner into taking an animal. Here's one she did yesterday.'

Caro took the piece of paper and read with amusement:

Laurel and Hardy, two friendly moggies desperately seeking country home. Will consider sharing with humans.

'Does it work?'

'Well, lots of people browse through the adverts and something like that just catches their eye. We've done quite well placing animals in the past month. Of course summertime is always tricky with people going on holiday, but we offer free kennel care for the first year.'

'And are they *all* strays?' Caro asked astonished. For such a small town it seemed like a lot of unwanted animals.

'Mostly; or abandoned kittens. Someone left a basketful on the doorstep last week. It makes me so angry. We offer a free neutering service, yet people just can't be bothered. Remember, every litter contains six or eight babies. I'm afraid we call ourselves a nation of animal lovers but people can be very irresponsible. I'd rather see a quarter of the cats in this country well cared for, than what we have today.'

Caro nodded sympathetically. Cats were not her favourite animals. Something about their lofty independence and disdainful eyes made her shiver, but she hated any cruelty to animals. Chucking pets out onto the street, having taken them on in the first place, seemed criminal to her.

'What would you like me to do?'

'Well, I'm afraid it's cage cleaning every morning, exercising, then medicine administration. You'll find the routine quite boring, dear.'

'I'm sure I won't,' Caro protested, determined to get stuck in and prove how useful she could be.

'Well, I'll introduce you to Sandy. Here, put these on,'

Pearl added, tossing a pair of rubber gloves to Caro.

They looked so old and grubby that Caro considered losing them somewhere, but when she saw the state of Sandy's hands she hurriedly put them on.

'Hi there!' Sandy smiled, pinning a strand of brown hair out of her eyes. She wore very old jeans and a check shirt. Caro, even in her oldest clothes, felt too clean and smart.

'Can I leave you to explain things?' Pearl asked. 'I'm off to the Cash and Carry.'

'No problem, see you.'

Caro watched Pearl trudge down the drive to her battered Land Rover, her hugely flowered skirt flowing brightly around her.

'If you watch me a minute you'll soon get the hang of things,' Sandy said, throwing back the double doors of the second shed.

It was a sad sight. Rows and rows of cages about three foot square faced a central aisle. By a clever arrangement of sliding doors, the cats could be let out of their pens at the back into the wired exercise areas. These were roughly fifteen feet long, on scrubby grass. The old scratching log and rubber tyre added minimal interest.

'Some cats like to be out together, others have to be kept separate. You'll get to know which soon enough. Now, this isn't a pleasant task but it has to be done. Waterbowls rinsed and refilled – there's a hose over there, then litter trays changed. If it doesn't look too dirty scoop out the worst then mix in fresh litter, otherwise start again. Some of the pens you'll have to hose out and leave to dry. I'm afraid not all cats are as clean as you'd expect. Persians are notoriously dirty. Think you can manage?'

Caro, whose nose had been curling, got a grip on herself and nodded confidently. It was a far cry from perfumed shampoos and mousse. She grinned at the idea of Elaine or even Michael up to their arms in cat mess. It wasn't a pleasant job by any standards, but there was a sense of satisfaction in getting cages clean for their returning occupants and spending a little time with each animal though, regrettably, far too little time.

Various characters were easily distinguishable. Some cats rubbed themselves against you, purring and fawning, revealing their soft underbellies, craving attention. Others hissed maliciously from the backs of their cages, lips drawn back, eyes shooting out sparks of pure hate. They were practically wild. 'That's why it's important to get them back into homes quickly. Of course the vicious-looking animals would not suit children, but with a single adult and the right environment they'd blossom,' Sandy explained, ruffling the head of a tortoiseshell who spat in return. 'Oh don't be so bad-tempered, Tootsie,' Sandy cooed, while Caro took a step back just in case those claws flew her way.

'We're getting on marvellously,' Sandy said, hands on hips, as she surveyed the final shed. 'And it's only half past eleven. Suppose I carry on here and you make some coffee?'

Caro trotted off happily. She'd put a lot of back-breaking work into cleaning and the smell of ammonia was making her eyes sting. Working with animals certainly wasn't all cute and soppy. She scrubbed her hands with excessive care and tried not to think of cat litter as she spooned sugar and coffee into two mugs. Ravenously hungry, Caro nevertheless didn't feel much like eating. She added extra sugar to her coffee instead and used the top of the milk to whiten it.

After the shortest of breaks, they finished the final cages, released the last few cats for exercise and turned their attention to medicines.

'The vet calls most weeks and gives his service free – we just pay for drugs. I don't know what we'll do when he retires. I doubt the majority of vets would be as generous. Anyway, it's mostly flea powders, boracic acid solutions for eyes, and jabs, which I can give.'

Caro crushed tablets into food and then learnt a canny method of de-lousing. Sandy filled a large paper bag with flea powder and scooped a cat into it, with just her head sticking out. Sandy rolled the cat gently under her arm and when released it was liberally dusted like a sponge cake in icing sugar.

'None in her eyes and not too much on me!' Sandy explained as Caro stared at the operation in astonishment.

Three cats with oozing eyes were treated with boracic solution. Far from stinging, it appeared to soothe and comfort the swollen eyes. Caro was careful to use fresh cotton wool on every eye to avoid transferring the infection. This job gave Caro enormous satisfaction. It was good to clean up a cat's eyes and watch her shake off the droplets of water hanging like dew on her whiskers.

'A cat's bite is dirty,' Sandy explained as she tended a war wound on a tom's back. 'Dogs have antiseptic bites, comparatively speaking, but if a cat is bitten by another it invariably turns septic.'

Caro found herself liking Sandy more and more. Without lecturing, she imparted useful and fascinating bits of information, leaving you wanting to know more or determined to research it yourself later. Caro began to wonder whether her science grades were good enough for her to apply to veterinary college. She, who had told everyone exactly what she wanted to do for a career, was now swapping her ideas on a daily basis!

After a relaxing lunch hour spent with a scraggy Persian cat on her knee, Caro answered a phone call from the local police station. Uncertain, she called for Pearl who was sorting out invoices from the morning's shopping.

'Do we take stray dogs?' she asked, hand over the receiver.

Pearl laughed. 'That'll be Sergeant Lewis. He always uses me as a last resort. Here, I'll speak to him.'

From the one-sided conversation, Caro guessed that the two, locked in amiable verbal battle, were old friends.

'It's cats, Lewis, not dogs. No, I won't. Oh very well. You'll owe me. In about half an hour. Bye.' Pearl looked red-faced but animated as she replaced the receiver.

'The Blue Cross Kennels are full, the RSPCA is too

busy, so it's me again. Come on, Caro. We'll take a drive down to Rattenhill Police Station.'

Caro jumped up, tipping the disgruntled Persian onto the floor. Cat hairs were an occupational hazard she decided, looking down at her lap ruefully. Pearl dragged a comb through her soft white hair, rubbed lipstick across her upper lip and then pressed her bottom lip onto it, blotting colour evenly if a little inaccurately. Caro wondered whether Lewis was also an admirer.

'There, that'll do. Bring a lead, Caro. There's several in that drawer.'

'What kind of dog is he?'

'Big and hairy according to the Sergeant! He's not much of an animal expert. It could be anything. The police don't keep animals any more. They haven't the facilities, so whoever has a spare place is contacted. Hopefully it'll just be lost and we'll have a frantic owner on the phone by this evening. On the other hand, Lewis says there's no collar so that could be bad news.'

'You mean it's been abandoned?' Caro cried, horrified.

'It happens – even to dogs.'

They were snarled up in lunchtime traffic through the centre of town, and Lewis was busy interviewing someone when they reported to the duty sergeant who knew nothing about a dog. They agreed to take a seat and wait. Caro had never been inside a police station before. Just sitting there made her feel guilty. It was daft but she kept expecting one of the WPCs to put a hand on her shoulder and lead her away. In the distance, a typewriter pinged and phones rang constantly.

At last a portly uniformed officer bore down on them and took Pearl's hand in a bear-like paw. 'Sorry to keep you waiting, my dear.'

'I'm only your dear when you have a favour to ask, you old rascal,' Pearl replied, but her eyes twinkled with fun. 'And what do you mean leaving us sitting here to all hours?'

'I've been interviewing a young lad – shoplifting. It's always the same, these lunch hours. They send kids out of school on this work experience lark and they're rifling the stores!'

Caro frowned primly and Pearl, catching her eye, laughed. 'You see, Caro, these old fogies tar the whole of the younger generation with the same brush. I'll have you know, Lewis, I wouldn't be here now if this young lady hadn't done such a fine job of work for me this morning. Work experience is an excellent idea.'

'Ah well, for some I suppose,' Lewis conceded. 'Now then, love, can you sign this and I'll get the beast for you. He's had three of my sandwiches and a pastie and he's still hungry, the poor old devil. I want him out of my office. The WPCs aren't doing any work – too busy playing with him!'

'Sounds better tempered than the last one you sent me, anyway,' Pearl remarked, as she followed Lewis into a side office.

Caro hesitated and then took her seat again. Pearl didn't need her trailing along. Feeling even more guilty now that she was on her own, Caro tried to look non-chalant and business-like. She wished her clothes didn't look so awful. It was a very odd sensation as business-suited men and women passed by, giving her that side-long glance that said, Oh yes, another troublemaker. What is it, shoplifting, truancy, trespassing? Caro reflected with interest how surprised and apologetic they would be if she'd said, 'Actually I'm here on business.' Funny how people always judged you on first impressions – how you looked or spoke and what you wore. Mind you, didn't she do that too? Caro was shocked from her thoughts by the sudden appearance of Simon and an older man being escorted out by a policeman.

'You're lucky to get off with a warning, you little moron,' the man snarled, landing a well-aimed clip to the back of Simon's head. He hardly flinched.

'Now, sir,' said the policeman, evidently embarrassed.

'I've lost an hour's pay through this!' the man continued, ignoring the officer and quite happy to make a scene in the busy foyer. 'You wait till I get you 'ome. I'll give you a tanning you won't forget.'

'You and whose army?' Simon taunted.

'Don't give my any lip, you miserable little toe-rag. Shoplifting – pah! Ain't you got the sense you were born with?'

'Sir, I must ask you . . .'

'All right, don't you shove me! I'm his father. I've got rights!' the man shouted, his mean dark eyes darting around for anyone to disagree with him.

Caro shrunk into her seat as they approached and wished she was invisible. Unfortunately at that moment Pearl erupted into the crowded foyer with a huge drooling collie-cross. 'Come on, Caro, let's get him home,' she boomed above the hubbub.

Caro got to her feet and found herself face to face with Simon's dad. She smiled feebly and edged around him, terrified of antagonising him further. Simon stared right through her, giving no sign of recognition at all. She hesitated for a second, unsure, but there was no point in communicating. So that was what he'd been doing when she covered for him. Shoplifting! Feeling sick and disgusted, Caro pushed past him out of the main doors. Sunlight hit her blindingly. Gulping fresh air, she chased after Pearl. She'd been right about Simon all along. Deep-down he was just an oaf, a cheat and a petty thief. Even his own father hated him. Good, I'm glad! Caro shouted inside her head. It helped block out the feelings of disappointment which rolled like a wave in her stomach.

A hot bath liberally doused with aromatic salt crystals had never felt so good, Caro decided, as she lay back just keeping her ears clear of the water. With freshly washed hair done up in a turban, Caro felt like an Eastern princess bathing in milk. She sipped from the mug of tea at her elbow and waggled her toes deliciously in the swirling bubbles. All the cares of the day also seemed to wash away with the grime and sweat. School was going to seem like a holiday camp after this fortnight. Caro blocked out the thought of the sixty-odd cages which it would be her lot to clean out again tomorrow. Surely some sort of automatic system could be designed so that . . .

'Caro, are you getting out of that bath tonight?'

'Coming, Dad. I'm soaking!' she shouted.

'Drowning, more like,' Caro's dad grumbled from somewhere on the landing.

With a sigh Caro flicked the plug out with her toe and reached for a clean towel. Once dry, she picked her dirty clothes up with two fingers and dropped them unceremoniously into the wash basket. At this rate she'd be out of old clothes before the weekend.

'Look at all this steam – it's like a sauna in here!' Mr McCarthy grumbled, passing his daughter as she floated by in her fluffy dressing gown.

'You're supposed to tell me how divine I smell,' Caro said in her sultry Hollywood star voice.

'It's better than how you smelt over supper at least! I suggest a bath *first* tomorrow.'

'Yes, well, if you'd had a homesick collie licking and slobbering up your arms *you* might not smell so sweet either.'

'Hm, I'll look forward to the hairdressing days then.'

'Not till next week I'm afraid,' Caro grinned, blowing him a kiss.

Downstairs, Caro's mum was watching TV and knitting. Caro had never understood how she could do those two things at the same time. If *she* took her eyes off a stitch for a second it got itself into amazing tangles or disappeared altogether. Helping herself to an apple, Caro subsided into the settee and let the box entertain her. The programme was just getting exciting when the phone rang. Mum started to put her knitting down, but her husband on his way downstairs picked the phone up first.

'Caro, it's for you.'

Puzzled, since she wasn't expecting a call from Lucy

or any of her other friends, Caro padded out to the hall.

'Who is it?'

'Some boy,' her dad said, giving her a knowing wink.

Caro snatched the phone from his hand, positive he was mucking around. It was bound to be Lucy.

'Caro, it's me, Simon.'

'Who?' She had heard correctly but it took a while for her brain to click into gear. What did he want at this time of night? Why would he call her at *any* hour?

'What do *you* want?' It sounded rude, which she hadn't intended it to.

'I need a favour.'

'Go on,' Caro said, highly sceptical.

'It won't cost you a thing,' Simon added. He sounded desperate, pleading.

Caro waited in silence. She wasn't going to help him.

'You know you saw me today?'

'Yes.' She forced herself to sound neutral.

'Well, if Michael checks up, can you tell him I was with Dad, only don't mention where.'

'Why should Michael check up with *me*?'

'Because I told him to.'

'You did *what*?' Caro stopped herself from shouting, aware that her parents could hear from the lounge.

'Listen, I needed to say something about being two hours late today. He wasn't taking the sick mum routine, so I had to say I was with my dad down the DHSS. I said the old man couldn't read – that's not far off the truth actually. Then I remembered you'd seen us – so I told him you'd vouch for me. He likes you.'

'I think you've got one hell of a nerve,' Caro hissed. 'Do you think I'm covering up for a thief?'

'You did yesterday.'

'I didn't know that's what you were up to yesterday!'

'Look, I don't want to get chucked out of this placement. I'll be expelled. That means no grades and no reference. I've gotta get out of my place next summer. I can't stand my dad any more. I need a job.'

'You should have thought of that before you went

41

shoplifting.'

'It's just kids' stuff, for a laugh. Everybody does it.'

'I don't.'

'Yeah, well maybe you don't have to. Look, I've finished with that now. I'm asking you, please.'

Caro dug her nails into her palm. She wanted to slam the phone down. He was waiting, expecting her to say no, to laugh and humiliate him.

'Can't your dad give you a note or phone or something?'

'My dad wouldn't spit to help me,' Simon said savagely. 'If Michael finds out I was caught shoplifting, he'll phone Mrs Clarke and that'll be that.'

'It's no more than you deserve.'

'I know.'

It was that simple, defeated acceptance that finally cracked Caro's resistance.

'This is the last favour I *ever* do for you, Simon. After this just keep out of my way. You're on your own.'

'You'll do it?'

'All right, but just listen, Simon, this *does* cost me. Despite what you might think, I don't enjoy lying and if I ever think you're still shoplifting, I'll tell everyone. Have you got that?'

'Loud and clear.'

'Right then, I'll see you on Monday.'

'Thanks.'

'I must be mad.'

'You're OK.' The phone went dead. Caro looked at the receiver for a while not quite believing the conversation they'd just had.

When the phone rang again about an hour later Caro was relieved to find that it was Mrs Clarke.

'Hello, Caro. How's your placement going?'

'Fine thank you, Mrs Clarke.'

'Good, good. Listen I've just had Mr Baines, your employer, on the phone.'

'Oh, really?' Caro said trying to sound innocent.

'Yes, about Simon. They've had problems with time-keeping I understand. Not that it comes as any surprise to me. Today was the last straw, I gather, but apparently Simon told some wild story about taking his father to . . .'

'Yes, I saw them there, Mrs Clarke, about half past two.'

'Oh, you did? So Simon hasn't been telling us all a pack of lies. Well, that alters things. Of course, the father isn't very supportive. Hm, perhaps I'll phone Mr Baines back and get him to reconsider. Thanks to your excellent work I *may* be able to persuade him to give Simon one more chance.'

'I think Simon would appreciate that. He's trying very hard.'

'Is he indeed? A surprise, frankly, but perhaps my advice has finally paid off. Well, I won't keep you, dear.'

Thankfully, Caro replaced the receiver. She felt that her quota of lies had been used for the next year. Still, if Simon really did stop shoplifting maybe it had been worth it.

'That phone must be red hot,' her dad remarked.

Caro smiled, grateful that her parents weren't given to prying. Sometime she would tell them all about it, but just now all Caro wanted was to be able to watch just one programme all the way through without interruptions.

'Can you make us some tea, Caro, while I explain these forms to Mr and Mrs Hill?' Pearl asked, looking up from her cluttered desk.

Caro slipped through to the kitchen and took extra care to choose cups without chips and arrange a tray neatly. It was their first answer to the advert and Caro found herself praying that the pleasant couple in the office would take a liking to at least one of the cats so desperately wanting a home. They had already explained that although the Laurel and Hardy advert had caught their eye, they really only wanted one cat. Caro had thought they would be immediately whipped through to the pens to make their choice, but Pearl had other ideas.

To begin with, they had to fill out a lengthy questionnaire, stating their past experience with cats, type of accommodation, proximity to roads etc.

'Some of our cats are city fellows and used to traffic, while others prefer the quiet life,' Pearl was explaining as Caro returned.

She balanced the tray on a stool and poured carefully to avoid slops.

'Now, do you have any preferences?' Pearl asked.

'Well, short-haired, I think, and not too old,' the lady said.

'But not a kitten,' her husband interrupted.

'Children?' Pearl enquired, her pen hovering in the air.

'All grown up.'

'Right, well we have a number who might be suitable. We operate on a trial basis, initially one month, and if there are any problems don't hesitate to phone. I'm happy to collect puss if you find he or she doesn't suit.'

Caro felt that Pearl wasn't trying very hard to encourage them to take an animal, but out in the shed Sandy explained why.

'It's no good placing a cat in an unsuitable home. They're either back with us or abandoned again within a week. That's no good for the cat or us. If people feel pressurised, they won't come and look. Pearl's quite shrewd about folk. If you make them feel they have to be fit to own a cat, they're more likely to make a good job of owning one. When a cat has been rejected more than once you can forget adoption. They never trust humans again. That's your trouble, isn't it, Tootsie?' Sandy said.

'I would *never* choose Tootsie if I came here,' Caro admitted.

'Well no, she doesn't look cute and friendly but just look at her. She's one of the best looking animals here. If anyone had the time to spend winning her over, she'd be a super pet.'

Caro was doubtful.

'I'd have her myself but she's a fighter. She'll be a one person cat,' Sandy predicted.

Caro was pretty sure she'd end up a no person cat but refrained from saying so. They watched as Pearl led the Hills from pen to pen, avoiding those she felt were unsuitable for their circumstances and the long-haired breeds. Sometimes they lingered smilingly before a cage then hurried past others. Caro felt herself tense with anxiety. She was keen that just one animal might be given a loving home tonight. Sensing that a decision was imminent, Caro sidled over towards Pearl to catch the conversation.

'I like that ginger. He seems so affectionate,' Mrs Hill said.

'Yes, that's George. He came to us after his owner had to go overseas. A very nice animal. About three years old.'

'What about him, dear?'

Mr Hill was studying a tortoiseshell three pens away. 'Come and look at this one.'

His wife reluctantly followed him. Pearl joined them. 'Max. Rather older than he looks; about eight I'd say. Been in a few battles but he's a bit past that now.'

'His ear is rather gnarled,' Mrs Hill objected.

'I think it gives him character,' her husband said defensively.

'Well, talk it over,' Pearl said placidly. 'There's no rush. We'll start the evening feeds, Caro.'

'Aren't you going to take them into the other shed?' Caro enquired.

'Goodness no. They're spoilt for choice as it is. If I give them any other cats to consider they won't be able to come to any decision.'

'Oh, I see.'

'They're having enough trouble as it is,' Pearl said, glancing back to the couple who were now in a heated debate outside Max's pen.

'I'll put my money on George,' Pearl whispered.

'I don't know, Max has a bit of fight left in him still,'

Caro grinned. They had fed nearly thirty cats before an apologetic looking Mr Hill came over.

'I'm sorry to be so long. We must have looked like a couple of squabbling children.'

'The important thing is making a decision you're both happy with. Is it to be George?'

'Or Max?' Caro asked, as he hesitated.

'Both, actually, if that's all right.'

'You did say you only wanted one,' Pearl reminded him. 'I don't want you to feel overrun.'

'We're quite settled now,' Mrs Hill said, hooking her hand in her husband's elbow. 'Two is just as easy as one. They'll be company for each other. They aren't fighters, are they?'

'Not with each other, happily.'

'Perfect,' Mr Hill said, patting his wife's hand.

Caro could have clapped with delight. She prepared two cardboard boxes for their transport, tucking a tin of food in each to tide them over. George went quite frantic when Mrs Hill cuddled him against her shoulder, purring like an engine and catching her hands between soft paws. Max was much more dignified and slightly indignant about missing his tea.

'That's a great end to the day!' Caro announced as the Hills drove away.

'They may be back,' Pearl warned.

'Oh, don't say that!'

'I've been in this job long enough not to let human nature surprise me,' Pearl said sagely.

It was the first time Caro had heard Pearl refer to her work as a job. Perhaps there was more to this expansive, generous lady than her cats.

They had just locked the sheds up for the night when a van drove up outside the office.

'That sounds like the RSPCA van,' Pearl sighed, pausing to listen. A door slammed and heavy feet crunched across the gravel. Someone rattled the door handle.

'Ah, thought I'd missed you.'

'Hello, Bill.'

46

The man, about thirty with tie and collar loosened, help up a battered cat basket.

'Am I going to like this?' Pearl asked.

'I don't think so.'

'Come on in.'

Caro took the basket from Bill and cautiously opened the catch. She caught her breath at the sight of what lay inside. Pearl peered in at the emaciated form of a black and white cat, one leg tightly bandaged. The dressings were new. The cat yowled but was evidently too weak to raise herself.

'Our vet's seen her. The leg's fractured. Been in an accident but otherwise she's OK. Badly undernourished of course. Not very old. I don't suppose . . .'

'As it happens we have a couple of spaces,' Pearl said, scooping the animal into her arms. 'But you'd better stay in the house tonight, hadn't you, my love, while we get some food into you.'

Caro noted the sagging skin and bony haunches with frustration. Her former feelings of elation sapped away. Pearl deposited the cat on an armchair and went off to poach some fish in milk to tempt the animal's delicate digestion.

'Don't look so despondent, Caro,' she called.

'But we've only just got rid of two and now . . .'

'Don't think of it like that. Three cats are better off now than they were this morning. Isn't that good news?'

'Yes, I suppose, but why are people so cruel?'

'Some are cruel, a lot are just ignorant. You have to keep pegging away and not get discouraged. That's what working with animals is all about – and people, come to that. Here, try her with this!'

Caro placed a dish of bread soaked in milk near the animal's nose. At first the cat ignored it, but at last she put out a tiny pink tongue and once started didn't stop until the dish was dry. She then set about licking her good paw.

'Hm, it looks like you're going to be OK, young lady,' Caro murmured, softly rubbing one ear.

The cat purred as noisily as a hive of bees.

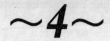

~4~

The weekend saw some of the worst weather experienced in the South West for several months. Gale force winds sent shipping scurrying for safe harbours, and several local sailing craft were battered against jetties or ripped from their moorings and lost down in the estuary. The local radio stations and newspapers were full of dramatic stories of rescue or disaster.

Apart from going to church on Sunday morning and getting soaked to the skin in the short walk from the car park, Caro and her parents spent a desultory weekend watching TV and pottering around. Caro started a piece of tapestry and gave up in under an hour. Her father went out to the garage to put up some shelves and soon had both his wife and daughter out there holding planks of wood while he drilled.

By the time Sunday evening arrived, Caro was glad that tomorrow she *had* to go out, whatever the weather. A shower of rain bouncing off the windows while you were cosy and warm inside was very pleasant, but this incessant, vicious downpour made you feel like a prisoner. The wind reached new peaks during the night and a loose window fitting kept Caro awake with its rattling until the early hours of the morning. When she awoke her limbs were heavy with fatigue and her eyes bleary.

'What a night!' Mrs McCarthy said at breakfast time.

'I've lost two of my chrysanthemums,' her husband announced, stamping the wet from his feet on the back door mat. 'Snapped off at the base.'

'At least the roof's all right. I was worried about the ridge tiles all night.'

'Yes, well, Mrs Tyler's lost a couple.'

'Oh dear, does she know?'

'Probably not. The curtains were still pulled.'

'I'll pop over later. I'd better phone Mr Black for her, though I expect he'll have enough to keep him busy for weeks after this weekend.'

'Tell her not to worry. I could probably fix them for her myself. I expect the ladder would reach. It's a two minute job once you're up there.'

Caro felt quite excited at the air of neighbourly support which this kind of trouble always brought out. All the way to the salon she saw shopkeepers conversing and helping each other sweep up rubbish or broken signs. Some shops had had their awnings ripped and workmen were busy clearing up before the first customers arrived. The modern uncluttered facade of Michael's had been left untouched by the cruel fingers of the storm.

Isobelle sat at the reception desk as glossily manicured and bejewelled as ever. Caro, whose hair had been blown into rain-streaked rats' tails and whose cheeks were wind-whipped and red, couldn't understand how Isobelle managed to appear so unaffected by the vagaries of the weather. Her hair never looked any different. It could have been moulded in bronze. Even the wispy hair framing her forehead looked designed.

'Hi,' she cooed, without raising her eyes from the copy of *Cosmopolitan* she was leafing through.

Caro, who had spent three days at the cats' home where people had to work in difficult conditions and not mind how they looked, now viewed the salon with fresh eyes. Michael's cool charm suddenly seemed rather false and Elaine's automatic smile a cover for her rather shallow, insensitive personality.

'Is Simon in?' she asked Isobelle as she hung up her raincoat.

'Um, came in early I think,' Isobelle returned.

Caro felt cheered by this piece of news. She'd managed her side of the bargain at any rate, and it looked as though he was keeping to his.

'Hello, Caro,' Michael smiled, 'I've got a lady waiting to be shampooed, but sort yourself out first.'

Caro glanced at her reflection in the mirror. Michael must mean the hair! Simon was nowhere in sight, presumably relegated to the storeroom again, which seemed silly as Caro was kept rushed off her feet by the constant stream of clients needing to be shampooed or removed from driers or made cups of coffee. She remembered that this was half term, a holiday they had given up in order to receive two weeks' work experience without missing two weeks of school at a crucial time. Of course, it would be busy with mums dragging children in to be appropriately clipped and tidied for the next half term.

Michael, looking bored, attacked a succession of boys wanting razor cuts, short sides and long fringes, army-type hair cuts, and then an equal number bullied into the shop by mums. They sat smouldering rebelliously while Michael removed the long strands so carefully nurtured for the past eight weeks. He quite obviously preferred his regular clients to this motley and unappreciative crew.

By lunchtime the wind and rain had picked up again and Caro decided to stay in the kitchen. Lucy would not be at the park and there was nothing worse than trailing round steamy shops in the wet. To her surprise, Simon joined her. He had a copy of *The Sun* and read it from cover to cover while drinking his coffee. Elaine, sitting at the table, sneered at his choice of reading matter with little pronounced sniffs. Caro watched her thumb through fashion magazines. She wondered whether Simon's unfriendly attitude was made worse by the people he was forced to work with and whom he quite obviously despised as much as they despised him. The atmosphere was not conducive to a relaxed lunch hour.

Caro noticed that Simon wasn't eating and wondered whether he'd had time to pack a lunch. She couldn't imagine his dad seeing him off with a lovingly prepared snack. If she offered to share hers, no doubt Simon would refuse. A more direct approach was required.

'Here,' Caro said, lobbing a Twix into Simon's lap. She didn't look at him, merely bit into an apple.

He studied the bar for a moment as if it might explode in his lap, then grunted, 'Ta,' and ripped off the wrapper.

Michael joined them. 'What a ghastly morning!' he whistled as he poured coffee.

Caro wasn't sure whether he was commenting on the weather or the clientele.

'At least it looks quieter this afternoon,' Elaine sighed.

'Well, that might give me time to offer one of you youngsters a free hairdo. Anything within reason of course.' Michael was obviously directing his comments at Caro. 'We've always offered it in the past to our work experience girls, so perhaps today is as good a time as ever before we lose you to the cats' home again.'

Caro smiled politely. There was no way anyone was getting near her head with a pair of scissors. Straight and long was how she liked her hair. No fuss, no frills and no spending hours done up like a porcupine. On the other hand, it was a generous offer and might be quite fun. Caro took a sidelong glance at Simon, his nose buried deeper in the paper.

'I think Simon would benefit from a haircut more than me,' Caro smiled.

'I've only got time for one of you today,' Michael said evasively.

'That's fine then, isn't it, Simon?' Caro said, daring him to object.

He opened his mouth to do so, but the expression of determination on Caro's face prevented him. It was blackmail, Simon decided, but probably he shouldn't push his luck. It might get the teachers off his back next week at any rate. Taking his sullen silence for assent Caro grabbed a warm towel and danced out to the basins.

'I'll wash, shall I?' she laughed, as Simon slowly folded his paper and trudged after her.

Michael, who hadn't intended to volunteer to cut the wretched boy's hair, froze the smirk on Elaine's face with a hard stare before wielding his scissors with an expert flick of the wrist.

'I suppose you think this is funny,' Simon hissed.

For reply, Caro forced his head back into the basin and directed very hot water on his head, narrowly missing his eyes.

'Ow!' he yelled.

'Don't be such a baby. You might look half decent with some of this lot off,' Caro teased, pulling at a long damp strand.

She gave him the full works – shampoo and conditioner – before throwing a clean towel in his face which he snatched and began scratching at his head.

'Ugh! It's all down my back.'

'You shouldn't have moved.'

'My scalp's half scalded.'

'Rubbish, it just hasn't seen water for so long. Michael's waiting,' she added sweetly. It suddenly occurred to her that, wet and tousled, his head from the back looked a bit like the collie they'd bathed the day Simon had been caught. The resemblance ended there. He was as irritable and moody as Tootsie.

'I *like* it long,' Simon said, as Michael whirled a sheet around his shoulders and tucked it in at the neck.

'Doubtless, but give me some credit for artistry,' Michael returned drily.

He combed Simon's hair deftly, tut-tutting at the jagged edges of the fringe which had been periodically and haphazardly chopped at various times in the past. Finally he began making huge swathes through the back of Simon's head, tossing the locks all over the floor. The dark hair quickly covered the pale blue tiles, and Caro went to fetch a broom before Simon noticed just how much was coming off and took fright.

At first it was hard to see Michael's design, but gradually the flashing scissors became more precise and the comb moved freely through very short, expertly layered hair. Drying more quickly now, the back moulded to the lines of the head was glossy, neat and tailored. Michael moved to the front, combing this way and that, searching for the natural wave and parting. Simon stared at his reflection poker-faced. Caro hadn't realised what a high forehead he had or how well-defined his eyebrows were. Short hair suited him. It made him look older, more responsible, more *handsome*. Caro surprised herself. That was a word she'd never have associated with Simon.

Michael took one or two casual snips at the fringe leaving it long, falling in that expertly managed, yet seemingly casual way that top stylists could manage. He rubbed gel in, slicked a comb quickly through it and then whipped off the sheet with a flourish. The transformation had taken barely fifteen minutes. Michael might not have much time for Simon but he was a true professional. It was a good job.

Caro clapped her hands, quite forgetting herself. 'Fantastic, brilliant. Doesn't it look great!' she whooped. Simon got up, looking acutely embarrassed. 'I feel like a ponce,' he muttered. Michael looked heavenward.

'Well, I think it's fabulous. Changes your image completely,' Caro said.

'Perhaps I liked my image as it was,' Simon returned.

'Rubbish. You look good, much better than . . .' Caro winced, biting her tongue. Why did she have to let her mouth run away with itself? 'Thanks, Michael,' she added.

'No problem. We'll see to yours later in the week. If not a cut an elaborate set perhaps?'

'That would be great, thanks.'

'Not at all, Madame,' he joked.

Caro watched Simon slink back to the kitchen with a sigh. He might have said thanks or shown *some* enthusiasm. He was such a misery guts. She had to laugh, however, when later in the afternoon she caught him flicking his fringe back with a comb as he passed a mirror. Whoever said girls took most pride in their appearance hadn't spent much time watching boys. They were just a bit more subtle about it.

Despite Elaine's assurances about a quiet afternoon, a brief let-up in the stormy weather brought out another set of mums and even Simon was ordered into the salon to keep the floors clear of clippings and maintain the flow of coffee. Caro washed hair until her fingers looked like prunes but still managed to keep up a string of polite conversation. Due to some oversight on Isobelle's part, a lady waiting for a cut and highlights had been booked in for too short a time. Elaine instructed Caro to wash the rubber cap used for the operation carefully and rattled out the number of the hair colourant required. Caro, in the middle of washing, didn't know whether to leave it or not. Catching Simon's eye she repeated the colourant number and pointed to the cupboard containing caps and cotton wool.

Caro was certain Elaine had said 6002, but when Simon handed her that bottle and she had cracked open the seal, the violet black liquid which gushed into the dish plainly wasn't the blonde lightener required.

'For goodness sake, boy, I said 6005. Can't you read?'

She whisked away to fetch the correct bottle leaving Simon scowling, obviously furious.

'I'm sorry, I was sure she said . . . Look, I'll explain,' Caro began.

'Oh for goodness sake, Caro. You're not my wet nurse! I *can* take care of myself you know. That silly woman wouldn't remember the time of day five minutes after checking her watch.'

'All right! I was only trying to help.'

'Yeah well, I'm not daft.'

'I know.'

'So leave it.'

'Simon, shampoo Mrs Taylor please,' Michael called.

Caro felt her knees turn to water. She knew Mrs Taylor, had heard her mum complain about her officious manner. If one drop of water went in her face there

54

would be no end to the fuss she'd create. It wasn't exactly fair of Michael, but she supposed everyone's nerves were frayed this afternoon. The coat-stand heaved with rain-coats and brollies, steaming uncomfortably in the heat of the driers wafting out from the salon. The perfumed hair was stifling. Caro wiped her damp forehead and sent another client towards the stylists' chairs. The woman picked her way through piles of hair with ill-concealed impatience.

'Simon, floor!' Michael called over his shoulder, picking up the thread of some conversation as easily as he'd dropped it.

'Anything else?' Caro heard Simon mutter, as he left Mrs Taylor at the basin and picked up the broom.

Caro would have attended to the client first, but Simon who was geared to a 'do as I'm told' mode this afternoon cleared the floor with great energy while Mrs Taylor knitted her brows and fumed silently. Simon's request for her to lift her feet while he swept under her chair more or less put the lid on it.

'Young man, I am *waiting* to have my hair washed. I have another appointment at four, so kindly put that broom down and attend to me.'

Caro was itching to go across and smooth things out, but Elaine had her holding the hair colourant while she tweaked strands through the bathing cap with a fine crotchet hook.

'Watch what I'm doing, Caro, I want you to finish this off,' Elaine murmured. Caro applied herself to the task in hand, reluctantly leaving Simon to his own devices.

It wasn't quite clear what happened but one thing was for sure. Simon was not entirely to blame for the tirade that Mrs Taylor poured on him as tepid water coursed down her pure silk blouse.

'I'm soaked!' she yelled, jerking forward so that another jet of water spurted in her ear.

Spluttering, she reached for the nearest towel and, eyes closed, grabbed the wet one Caro had left over the next chair. Thoroughly irritated, Mrs Taylor threw it in disgust on the floor and demanded to see the manager, by which, she told Elaine, she meant Michael, not some girl!

'I didn't know the water was cold,' Simon defended himself. 'Anyway if she hadn't moved it wouldn't be down her flippin' blouse.'

'Be quiet!' Michael barked. 'Now, Mrs Taylor, allow me to finish your shampoo. Towels, Simon!' he added snapping his fingers.

'Just a minute!' Mrs Taylor said, not in the least mollified. 'That boy was both insolent and loutish. I pay good money here, as you well know, and I expect decent service. How can you employ riff-raff like this and expect to maintain standards?'

'Mrs Taylor, the boy is on work experience and . . .'

'Not a particularly astute choice for a boy of his type I would think.'

'You're dead right!' Simon yelled, unable to contain himself any longer. 'I must be flippin' mad panderin' round silly old biddies like you.'

'Simon!' Michael said. Caro thought he was going to faint. Mrs Taylor was hyperventilating. 'Right that's it, you're out!'

'Fine!' Simon tossed back, as he dropped his apron on the ground and slammed through the kitchen doors.

There was a terrified silence in the salon until some girls started to titter, and a couple of women at the stylists' tables exchanged knowing glances and started talking about how they blamed the teachers.

'It sounds as if he got what he deserved,' Lucy observed. She was sitting cross-legged on Caro's bedroom floor, flipping through knitting and crochet patterns. Crochet tops were all the rage again and Caro's mum had promised to get them started if they chose something simple.

Caro was barely concentrating. Her mind was too full of the injustices of the afternoon. She had come away with £3 in tips and another £5 from Michael who said they'd never have managed without her hard work. It felt like blood money.

'I bet he only gave it to me so I wouldn't tell Mrs Clarke about the way Simon got fired.'

'You're not still on about that money are you?' Lucy moaned. 'Give it to *me* if it's going to worry you that much. You earned it, didn't you?'

'Yes, but I still feel rotten about what happened to Simon. Michael *knew* it wasn't his fault as well. He only fired him because he was frightened of Mrs Taylor.'

'Well, from what your mum said maybe we'd have done the same thing. Her husband's a leading councillor. Michael's hardly going to upset her – planning permission for extending the premises you know.'

'Oh, you sound like my dad. I'm sure it's not all as corrupt as he makes out.'

'I wouldn't put it past them. My mum always says it's not what you know, it's who you know.'

'In that case it stinks!'

'You'll be able to change it, Caro, when you're up there in your plush office wheeling and dealing!'

Lucy couldn't resist rubbing it in about Caro's previous aspirations now that a lot of her illusions had been so roughly shattered.

'Actually money comes into everything. You know my nursery? Well, they charge £200 a month to keep a toddler there during working hours Monday to Friday.'

'That's a lot,' Caro agreed.

'You have to earn a heck of a lot to afford it, but if you can't afford it, you can't work, so you end up on supplementary benefits. One woman has stopped sending her little boy there because she's worse off working, paying for the nursery, than staying at home and claiming the dole. Daft, isn't it?'

Caro tried to show interest, but her mind kept returning to Simon.

'Perhaps if I phoned Mrs Clarke and explained?'

'She'll think you've got a crush on him or something the way you're taking all this trouble,' Lucy commented drily.

'Don't be silly!' Caro flashed, aware even as she said it that her protest was a bit too strong. 'Don't you see, he's going to get dropped from all the exams now and he's so desperate to get a job next year. He doesn't stand a hope without some kind of reference.'

'Caro, this time not even *you* can wave a magic wand. I'm afraid that's the last we've seen of Simon Mitchel. You did your best, in fact a lot more by the sound of it. Now can we take a proper look at these patterns, or shall I go downstairs and talk to your mum?'

Caro slid off the bed and pulled the pattern books towards her. Lucy was right, it was no good going on about something that had no remedy. It was just a pity that the moment they'd struck up *some* sort of understanding, fate stepped in to make sure they'd never see each other again. It was a funny old life. The worst thing was that, with nothing to aim for now, Simon would have every excuse to slide back into shoplifting or worse. She shuddered.

'Are you cold? Shall I close the window?' Lucy asked.

'It *is* closed – you'd never think so, the draught that gets by that loose catch. Dad's promised to do it for months, and now the screws have pulled out of the wood so it'll be a major repair job. Mum gave him a real go over it at tea time.'

'Your mum and dad *never* argue,' Lucy said, seriously. 'If you want to hear rows come round my house. You're lucky, Caro.'

Caro made a vow to remember that. It was true that her parents rarely fought. The house was usually peaceful and happy. You tended to take it for granted, but Caro was beginning to understand some of the give and take that went into a happy home. God came into it as well. She knew her parents spent time together talking abut everything, including their faith. When Dad had gone into business on his own, Caro's mum had been dead set against it, but she'd later admitted that after talking to a couple of people at church and praying about it, things had looked entirely different. Now, it was Mum

58

suggesting that they take on new lads, instead of her father.

'Do you reckon God can look after people for you, if you ask?' Caro said.

Lucy considered this for a moment. 'You mean like people going on journeys?'

'Well, maybe. I mean we all wish people a safe journey, don't we, and say things like "God bless".'

'I don't think that's a guarantee of no travel accidents. I mean, people must have said that when planes crash or trains are derailed. You can't guarantee there won't be accidents.'

'So why bother saying it?'

'Well, it's sort of comfortable, isn't it? It shows you're going to think about the person and they're in God's hands, so to speak.'

'Even if the plane comes down?'

'Well, yes. God is everywhere after all.'

'Do you *feel* that God is with you?' Caro asked, pressing Lucy for a definite answer.

'Of course.'

'Sometimes *I'm* not sure he's there at all. Like this afternoon, where was he when Mrs Taylor came in?'

Lucy giggled. 'Were you expecting a celestial angel to guide the water hose in Simon's hand?'

'Don't make fun!'

'Well, what do you expect, Caro! God isn't there to pick up banana skins and divert traffic round corners so it won't mess up your afternoon ride.'

'OK, then, so why expect God to do anything at all? I'm just trying to work out what we mean when we leave things in God's hands. Are we just shirking our responsibilities?'

'We're still talking about Simon, aren't we?'

'Not necessarily but, all right then, let's suppose we are.'

Lucy thought for a moment, weighing her opinions, remembering things she'd ever been told or read.

'OK then, think about this. You're convinced that it's

the end of the line for Simon because, for whatever reason, he's messed up this placement.'

'Which I've been slogging myself out to keep him in,' Caro nodded.

'But supposing this was the wrong placement anyway? Supposing there's a much better opportunity just round the corner that you wouldn't have a clue about, or not even Simon knows about, come to that.'

'So God planned this afternoon's fiasco?' Caro looked horrified.

'No, not at all. It's just that we always think there's one right way through life and every failure or messed up bit is going to be a lifelong disaster. It isn't. There are hundreds of ways we could each live our lives and God would be there whichever we chose, I'm sure of it.'

'How do you mean?'

'Well, look at our placements. You hated the idea of both placements, yet you reckon they've been really useful, in their own ways.'

'They've changed my mind about going into business certainly.'

'There you are then. You believed God would be with you in the bank if you'd been put there. Why not believe he's also at the salon or the Cats' League?'

'You mean he's following me, rather than the other way round?'

'I mean he's everywhere we go. If I told you to walk to the shops, you could walk two ways. One is a bit longer but you'd still get there. I think life's like that. There might be quick ways, long ways, dull or dramatic ways, but you can still find God *all* the way and I'm sure there are hundreds of choices at every stage which we could make. It needn't alter the end result, which is learning to live as a Christian and helping whoever we can along the way. You did what you could for Simon, now it's someone else's turn.'

'So leave him in God's hands?' Caro smiled.

'That's about it.'

'Will you help me pray for Simon right now, just in

case he's about to go shoplifting?'

Lucy laughed out loud. 'You're just a bossy, interfering woman!' She dodged a pillow before they settled down to pray that wherever Simon was, or whatever he was doing or thinking, God would be around him.

'I feel a lot better about it now,' Caro said, 'and I think that pink top, done in jade, would suit you perfectly.'

'Oh, I've got your attention at last! Come on then, let's go and see what your mum thinks. Knowing my luck I'll have picked the most complicated pattern in the book.'

'You'd better hope the fashions don't change by next year then,' Caro laughed.

'Very funny, come on.'

'Oh that window!' Caro gasped, as they opened the bedroom door causing a through draught. 'It'll be off its hinges if this wind keeps up.'

Downstairs Caro's parents were watching the news and held up a warning finger as the girls bounced in noisily.

'Sh, there's a newsflash, something about a grounded oil tanker.'

The main points of the evening news were repeated before a few brief lines were devoted to information just coming in of stormy conditions off Plymouth Sound forcing an Iranian oil tanker onto the rocks at St Budle beach.

'That's only just along the coast!'

'Sh!'

'Oil is already seeping out and environmentalists are predicting heavy pollution to beaches and wildlife. So far, storm conditions are making assessment of the situation difficult. We will keep you up to date with any new developments. Now the stock exchange and on a busy day . . .'

'Turn to the local news,' Caro said, pouncing on the remote control. 'Oh, we've missed it.'

'There'll be more on later, bound to be,' Mr McCarthy said.

'Another beach ruined,' his wife sighed, 'and all those poor birds.'

'You'd think they'd find safer ways of containing oil . . .'

'Or better methods of cleaning it up. Oh, here we are, another news flash.'

The local reporter, staggering against the wind, had little extra information although early pictures already showed the tell-tale signs of massive pollution to follow. One or two birds badly covered in oil flapped just feet away from the reporter. It was a sad and frustrating scene. The report ended with requests for volunteer help once the clean-up operation could begin.

'Let's hope this wind abates during the night,' Mr McCarthy sighed.

'Can we join in the clean-up?' Caro demanded.

'Well, would we be much use?' her mum said doubtfully.

'Anyone can shovel oil, I suppose,' Lucy said.

'You'll volunteer, won't you?' Caro demanded.

'Well, yes, if they can use me,' Lucy replied.

'That's settled then,' Caro said, her eyes bright with determination.

Mr McCarthy couldn't think where that organisational streak came from.

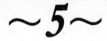

~5~

News of the oil slick was all over the local newspapers
by the next morning and had even merited a mention on
the front page of the national paper which Mr McCarthy
always liked to read over breakfast. Local radio broad-
casters were issuing up-to-the-minute news flashes from
rescue service officials on the scene, but the messages
were depressing. Strong winds continued to batter the
coast, driving yet more oil onto beaches where birds
seeking refuge from the storm were trapped.

'Why don't they start spraying the slick or something?'
Caro demanded. 'It's no good just standing around talking about it.'

'With the weather as it is, spraying might do more
harm than good. Although it's going to make a mess of
Budle Beach, at least it may miss Tor Bay if it stays
together,' Mr McCarthy said, as he started on his second
slice of toast.

Caro pushed her cereal bowl aside with a sigh. All
those lovely birds dying and no one could do a thing until
the weather improved. So much for modern technology.

'Won't you be late?' Mrs McCarthy warned, waving
a buttery knife in the direction of the kitchen clock.

'I'm on my way. Listen, if you hear anything about
the Youth Club going out to help clean up, make sure

you get the details.'

'Will do. Have a good day. Don't forget your lunch.'

'Oh, ta, Mum.'

As Caro battled against the wind, she felt a rising anger against whoever was responsible for letting such a disaster befall her favourite beach. A car horn tooted at her as she took a step off the kerb. The traffic was heavier than usual, a steady stream of vehicles belching out carbon monoxide driven by frustrated workers leant over the wheel in case half a car's length should suddenly open up in front of them. We're all responsible, Caro thought. How many times did her own parents use the car when they could have walked, or drive alone rather than share? Cars drank gallon upon gallon of petrol, demanding more and more oil production. What were a few birds compared to the financial dealings of the oil producers? When you came down to it, there wasn't much point in blaming one poor captain whose ship had just happened to get caught in rough seas on a dangerous coastline.

Caro stopped walking and paid attention to her where-abouts. Idiotically, she'd just passed Michael's. Hurrying to retrace her steps, Caro didn't see the figure jogging in the opposite direction. They collided with such force that Caro was sent spinning, landing painfully on one knee and grazing her hands. The figure rushed forward to help her up, full of muttered apologies.

'Oh, it's you!'

Caro, whose eyes were watering with the pain of her sore hands, focused properly and recognised Simon's face peering anxiously into hers. The new hairstyle had really altered his features, softened them somehow.

'Can you get up?' he asked, still full of concern, which somehow surprised her.

'Yes, I'm fine,' she lied, feeling a bit wobbly. The fall had winded her.

'Off to Michael's?'

'Yes, of course. I'm sorry about the other day. You didn't deserve that.'

'I probably did. I deserve most of what I get. Anyway

I ought to be thanking you. I'd have been gone long since without your help.'

'It was nothing. Look, why don't you see Michael yourself? I'll help you explain. He was only intimidated by that stupid woman. I'm sure he'd change his mind if . . .'

'Forget it, Caro. It wasn't my line anyway.'

'But your references . . .'

'I know, that's a pig, but it can't be helped. Look are you OK, because I was in a bit of a hurry myself.'

'School?'

Simon laughed expressively. 'I'll see you around, maybe.'

'Yes, I hope so,' Caro returned and found herself meaning it. She wished she knew where he was going in such a hurry. More shoplifting? It was all too likely. She limped into Michael's painfully.

It seemed like the longest morning in creation. Elaine was quite kind about her hands, searching out plasters and ensuring that the stylists did most of their own shampooing, but that left very little to while away the hours. Caro had made such an impact on tidying during the early part of her placement that, apart from relieving Isobelle on reception for twenty minutes which she enjoyed, there was only feeding the tumble drier to do. Even this might have been tolerable if the pressing matter of the oil slick hadn't been in Caro's mind and occupying all her thoughts. The trivial salon chit-chat was unbelievably irritating. Isobelle hadn't even *heard* about the disaster and Elaine didn't remember ever going to Budle Beach.

'Is it sandy?' she asked.

'Well yes, but there's a lot of rock pools too, and you have to climb down steps built against the cliffs.'

'Oh well, I won't have been then. I can't stand beaches unless there's lots of sand and you can walk straight from the car park onto the beach. And if it's all going to be tar now I definitely won't bother. Thank goodness I booked Tenerife early for my holidays. This will send all the West Country grockles abroad.'

That seemed to be the limit of Elaine's interest in the matter. A few customers chatted about the problem, but everyone seemed to think it was 'one of those things' you just had to sigh about and accept. Caro wanted to do more, a lot more. Why didn't people cause more fuss about the destruction of their own countryside? There was an uproar if vandals dumped litter in private gardens, but the complete devastation of miles of coastline seemed to leave people unmoved. More aggravated mothers towing unwilling youngsters into the salon rounded off a tortuously boring morning. Caro couldn't wait to get to the cats' home. At least you could have an intelligent conversation with Sandy.

Before lunch, Caro helped Michael with a perm. The client was deaf, so even Michael's charms and wit were wasted on her and he rolled papers into sections of hair in silence. Caro had been thinking about what Pearl had said about relying on sponsorship so she decided to approach Michael on the subject. His was a successful business. He could surely afford a little charity.

Michael's response was more or less as Caro had predicted, but his reasoning annoyed her.

'This is still a fairly young business as I'm sure you realise, and I have a lot of overheads, so sponsoring anyone else would be something I'd have to think hard about.'

'The Cats' League is an excellent cause though,' Caro urged, 'and it wouldn't do any harm for a business based on vanity to be seen to be connected to a venture which actually relieves suffering.'

Michael seemed a little put out by Caro's description of his vocation, but he smiled evenly and appeared to give her idea some thought.

'You may have a point, Caro. Well done, but I think when I decide to sponsor it will be something a little more glamorous than a home for flea-bitten moggies! I have to think of the image of this place, you see. We're attempting to create an aura of elegance and sophistication. If I were to sponsor a health club or beauty salon, then there would be financial spin-offs for me as well. That's what good sponsorship is all about. Nobody just gives money away. You'll soon learn that when you get into your own business.'

'I don't think I'd be much good in business,' Caro said, stiffly. She was quietly seething about Michael's selfish, hard-headed attitude over sponsorship.

'On the contrary, I think you'd be marvellous.'

Caro didn't know whether to be flattered or insulted. There was no way she wanted to be tarred with the same brush as Michael, the successful businessman. Surely there was room for charity and understanding in business? If there wasn't, she wanted no part of it.

At last one o'clock arrived and Caro was free. Pearl wouldn't be expecting her until two but, suspecting that she might have been called out to deal with sea birds, Caro decided to eat her lunch on the bus rather than take a lunch break.

Pearl was pleased to see her early. 'It's all hands on deck today!'

'I wondered whether you'd be out collecting oiled birds.'

'I haven't needed to – my colleagues from animal rescue have already delivered our quota of convalescents. Come and see.'

In three empty cat pens about a dozen tar-streaked heron gulls sat on pieces of old sacking. Their yellow eyes flashed menacingly but their ruffled, filthy plumage was pitiful.

'Is that as clean as you could get them?' Caro asked, instantly aware of how rude this sounded.

Pearl's eyes wrinkled as she hooted with laughter. 'And there was I thinking what a good job we'd done!'

'I'd like to see you do better,' Sandy grunted, appearing from a neighbouring row of pens.

'Oh I didn't mean . . .' Caro began, flushing with embarrassment.

'Don't worry. Most people have that reaction. They

assume cleaning feathers is easy but it's not. There are no magic solutions. It's just plain old detergent and warm water. With that beak to watch it's a tricky job, and it's no good getting them too stressed or they could die anyway. After a night's rest we'll see if any more oil can be got out.'

'And then they're released?' Caro asked.

'Not quite. The detergent also removes all the natural oils which protect their plumage and give them buoyancy. They need time to produce more if they're to stand any chance of survival.'

'What will you feed them on?'

'Cat food seems to be going down quite well. It *is* fish variety!'

'Don't the cats worry them?'

'Even Tootsie would have met her match with these birds!' Pearl laughed. 'We'll try to keep as quiet as possible and leave them in the dark. With any luck they'll look more perky by this evening.'

'They won't die, will they?' Caro asked anxiously.

'I hope not. It depends how much oil they ingested before being picked up. As they attempt to clean themselves, the oil poisons them from inside. It really is hopeless for them unless they're caught early.'

'Were many birds saved?'

'Well, the RSPB team took charge of the rarer breeds. There were some cormorants and a pair of shags that they were particularly concerned about. As usual, I took pity on the common underdogs. Several dozen had already died of course. Goodness knows how many more there will be. The beach was covered when the rescuers got down there this morning, by all accounts.'

'I'm going down this evening,' Caro said. 'There must be some way I can help.'

'We'd better get these cats fed then, if you want to be away on time.'

Caro flung herself into the work, ignoring Sandy's calls at tea break, to try and make up for the time the other two had been forced to spend on the birds that morning. For all the good she'd done at Michael's it would have been more useful to have been here all day. Not for the first time, Caro was viewing her placement at the cats' home as far more valuable than her experience at Michael's. Perhaps she was beginning to realise where her priorities lay. Caro recalled her warning to Lucy about doing a job which was so financially unrewarding. Lucy had replied that money didn't matter, and Caro had to agree now that it wasn't the be-all and end-all. Pearl wasn't smart or charmingly mannered, but she was worth a hundred smooth-talking businessmen who only cared about profits and costs. Pearl also seemed to get a lot more fun out of life than people like Isobelle or Elaine, who were constantly worried about their nail varnish and making snide comments about people behind their backs. Funny how all your ideas could be turned on their head in a week, Caro thought.

'That was your mum on the phone,' Sandy said, appearing with a mug of tea.

'I didn't hear the phone,' Caro said, straightening to refasten a pen.

'You've been moving like a whirlwind down these cages!'

'I wanted to get them done. What did she want?'

'Just to let you know that the Youth Club is meeting at Budle Beach to join in the cleaning up operation. Pearl says you're to take a break. I'll finish here.'

'I'm all right, honestly.'

'I know, but you'll need *some* energy left for tonight. Thank goodness the wind has died down. They've managed to get tugs out to the tanker and hope to get her upright. At least that will stop any more oil being spilled. Apparently there's quite a party atmosphere down there. All sorts of groups have volunteered to help, and the council have commandeered some tractors to help shift dirty sand.'

'Great. At least something's being done.'

'Yes, these things always take a while to organise.'

Caro felt whacked by the time she'd changed and eaten

tea. Lucy arrived at six looking fresh as a daisy, wielding her dad's shovel and a pack of refuse sacks.

'This is what Kate ordered!' she replied in answer to Caro's question.

'I thought we were saving the wildlife.'

'We are – the prevention method!' Mr McCarthy said appearing through the back door with two more shovels. 'Are you ready?'

Caro nodded, gulping down one last mouthful of coffee.

The car park behind Budle Beach was half full when they arrived. From a distance, the anorak-hooded figures trailing back and forth along the water's edge with spades or sacks looked like children building sand castles. The Youth Club and several parents had gathered around the Strides' battered old Volvo, from the boot of which Kate was doling out sandwiches and coffee.

'The toddlers' club had a birthday party,' she explained, 'and there were loads of sandwiches left over. I thought we could use them. It's not really beach weather though.'

Caro hunched her shoulders against the biting wind and closed her mouth as a swirl of sand smacked into her face.

'Ugh! Revolting!' Lucy moaned.

'I think that's everyone,' Peter Stride said, peering over the heads of the assembled group. 'Now, I've had a word with one of the organisations here and they suggest we take the far rock pools. I'm afraid it's a matter of scraping off the surface layer of shingle, bagging it and dumping. There are several skips around. Mind out for tractors. I've got a few tools here if anyone's come without. Good luck!'

The scramble down the steps to the water's edge was heartbreaking. Great clots of oil lay everywhere, like the stinking blood of some awful sea monster. The blackened shapes of dead birds were dotted up and down the beach. Any that were still alive had apparently been gathered. There was no point in feeling morbid over what couldn't be helped, however, and the two friends made their way quickly to the rock pools which were deserted.

'You shovel, I'll hold the bag, then we'll swap over,' Caro decided quickly. They worked methodically, quickly realising that hauling half a bag of sand to the skip was easier than dragging a full one. At last, they got into the swing of it and began to see clean patches of sand appearing at their feet. The rocks could only be skimmed off with hand trowels, but at least most of the glutinous muck was removed, making the rocks less of a hazard to birds. Straining oil off the surface of the water trapped in the pools was trickier, but Lucy had a brilliant idea of using a bag to drag across the surface and then sloshing the contents over a shovel of dirty sand. The oil stuck while the water drained out.

Without the encouraging fact of so many knots of people all pegging away on the fringes of the beach and the growl of tractors pacing up and down in the centre, the task would have seemed hopeless but, as the light began to fade, there was a definite sense of achievement in the air. Oil still lay around but there *were* gaps and these, in places, had grown appreciably in the three hours they had been working.

A distant whistle halted the council workers who turned the head-lights of their tractors towards the car park.

'Shall we call it a day?' Lucy asked, pushing a dark damp curl out of her eye.

'One more bag,' Caro said.

'You're the boss!' her friend smiled, stooping to hold the bag upright.

'Sorry, am I still pushing you around? I ought to have learnt my lesson after this week,' Caro sighed apologetically.

'I was only joking.'

'But you're right. I'm always throwing my weight around. Is it sickening?'

'Of course not, stupid!' Lucy said, prodding her friend lightly on the shoulder. 'Anyway, I like being organised.

People like you are natural leaders – you can't help bossing everyone else around!'

Caro looked up with a worried frown, but caught the twinkle in Lucy's eyes just in time. 'You're a swine, Lucy Baker!'

'I have to keep you from getting too high and mighty some of the time, that's all.'

'Well, I'll let other people get on with their own lives in future.'

'Still thinking about Simon?'

'Not really. Mind you, I saw him this morning. Bumped into him quite literally, actually.'

'On some crowded street, your eyes met. He rushed across . . .'

'Shut up!' Caro said. 'It wasn't like that. I wish I'd never mentioned it to you.'

They worked in silence for a moment or two before Lucy's curiosity got the better of her. 'Go on, then. What did he say?'

'Nothing, he was just . . .'

'What? Don't be so cagey, it's infuriating!'

'I don't know, he seemed nicer, that's all.'

'Mitchel, *nice*! That's a bit hard to swallow.'

'Well, don't get too excited. He was off somewhere in a steaming hurry and it wasn't school, which is where he should be going, seeing as his placement has fallen through.'

'To be lectured by Mrs Clarke. I'm not sure even I'd feel up to that.'

'But why can't he toe the line like other people? I bet he was off shoplifting – bound to be.'

'Hang on Caro,' Lucy laughed. 'Aren't you jumping the gun a bit? You don't *know* that at all.'

'Well, it's the kind of thing he *would* be doing,' Caro grumbled, tipping the last shovelful of polluted sand in the bag.

'You've put too much in now. We'll never carry it,' Lucy predicted.

'Well, I'm not taking any out now. We'll just have to

drag it. Grab your end.'

After twenty paces the girls subsided onto the sand in exhaustion.

'Slave-driver!' Lucy panted. 'Your bright ideas'll be the death of me.'

'Need a hand?'

A man in a green waxed jacket and tweed cap bent to upend the collapsed sack and deposit it in the skip some fifty feet away.'

'Thanks,' Caro gasped, trotting to keep up with him.

'Don't mention it. I've been watching your group. You've made quite an impact on that section of the beach.'

'Well, every little helps, I suppose. Are you with an official group?'

'Greenpeace. We've been here all day.'

'Gosh, you must be exhausted!' Lucy said.

'Hungry! Some of us haven't eaten since breakfast.'

'Do you want some sandwiches? Our minister's wife brought hundreds and most of us had already eaten before we arrived.'

'That would be very kind if you think they can be spared. By the way, my name's Roger. I'll introduce some of my other helpers in a minute.'

'Meet us up in the car park when you've finished,' Caro suggested. 'It's a green Volvo.'

'I'll follow my nose,' Roger said.

'Come on, Lucy, we'd better warn Kate,' Caro said, as they watched Roger disappear back to his group.

'What a nice man.'

'Yes, it's funny how much friendlier people are in the midst of a disaster.'

'All for one and one for all! Wouldn't it be great if people were like this all the time, but without the need for a disaster.'

Kate Stride wasn't in the least put out by the arrival, some minutes later, of a dozen young women and lads with raging appetites bearing down on the picnic hamper in the boot of the Volvo. The much depleted stocks of food somehow held out even though the coffee had long since run dry. The members of Greenpeace, mostly in their twenties, had helped council workers clear a large part of the main beach.

'Usually we find ourselves demonstrating against the council or local business, so it's quite refreshing to be on the same side for once,' Roger explained to Peter Stride.

'Come on, dear, you must be able to manage another one of these,' Kate Stride said to a younger lad standing away from the others.

'Simon's got hollow legs,' Roger shouted cheerfully, 'he'll eat anything that's going!'

At the name, Caro involuntarily looked up. It couldn't be the same.

'Hey, look over there. Isn't that Simon Mitchel?' Lucy said, pointing. 'Oh, no, it can't be. The hair's too short.'

'It is!' Caro hissed. 'Don't stare with your mouth open.'

'I thought you said he'd be shoplifting,' Lucy whispered, enjoying her friend's discomfort.

'All right, don't rub it in. So I was wrong. Well, thank goodness I was. I'm pleased to see him here. It just doesn't seem the sort of thing Simon Mitchel would get involved with.'

'Aren't you going to talk to him?' Lucy demanded.

'Don't want to embarrass him.'

'Why should you? You're *shy* of him.'

'I am not.'

'Talk to him!'

'No!' Caro hissed.

'Well, I will then,' Lucy replied and made her way over.

'Hi there. Didn't expect to see you! Are you a member of Greenpeace?'

'Oh, hi. Yes, sort of. I just come along when they need manual labour.'

'Caro's here too,' Lucy informed him. It was hard to judge for any reaction in the twilight.

'This your church then?'

74

'Part of it.'

'Didn't think churches did this sort of thing.'

'It's not all prayers and singing hymns, you know,' Lucy joked.

'No, I guess not.'

'Been here all day?'

'Yep. Hell of a lot more useful than work experience.'

'Oh,' Lucy responded casually. Better not to let on that Caro had been talking about him to all and sundry. 'I'm having a great time at the nursery.'

'It's OK if you got what you wanted.'

'Caro didn't.'

'Yeah, well, she'd get on all right anywhere, wouldn't she.'

Lucy couldn't quite decide whether the tone of that comment suggested a compliment or scorn.

'Have you got a lift home?' she said, noting the thin jacket sticking to his shirt was damp.

'I'll walk, or get a bus.'

'Well, Caro's dad brought us in the car. Shall I ask if he can squeeze you in?' Lucy wasn't in the habit of offering favours from other people, but she felt a sudden rush of sympathy and concern for this boy who devoured dried-out cheese sandwiches as if they were the best thing he'd tasted all week.

He shook his head firmly. 'I'm OK.' The guarded look warned Lucy not to interfere. He didn't need or want charity. They stood in awkward silence for a moment before Lucy launched into a new stream of conversation. It was a little while before she realised that he wasn't paying attention and, tracing his glance, she noticed with a smile that he was watching Caro who was chatting to Roger.

Lucy made her way back to her friend with a smug knowing look.

'Go and offer him a lift,' she said, as soon as they were on their own.

'Why?'

'He needs one. I offered but he said no.'

'Well, then.'

'But he'd say yes to you.'

'Rubbish.'

'He *would*. He likes you.'

'Lucy Baker, you do talk rubbish sometimes,' Caro said crossly.

'You're getting touchy.'

'I am *not*,' Caro retorted, touchily.

'I thought you were the one getting all worried about him.'

'I was, but he'll just think I'm being patronising.'

'So, you'll let him walk home in all this weather?'

'If he wants to. It's his choice. Anyway, it'd be dead embarrassing after all the things I've said about him to mum and dad. They think he's a real yob.'

'So do you.'

'No, I don't any more.'

'You thought he was shoplifting this morning.'

'Well, I was wrong and I don't need you to make me feel any worse about it, thank you.'

Lucy smiled, having made her point. She was extremely fond of her friend, but it didn't do Caro any harm to have to re-evaluate her ideas and opinions once in a while.

Unwittingly Mr McCarthy solved the problem by asking Roger if anyone needed a lift. Roger promptly called Simon over and the matter was settled. Caro spent one of the most uncomfortable and agonising journeys of her life wedged between Lucy on her left who smirked like a Cheshire cat the whole time, and Simon on her right who had trouble with his long legs and kept apologising every time his knee accidentally touched hers. To top this, Caro dreaded her mum asking too many questions. She wasn't sure whether they had worked out that this was *the* Simon.

Predictably, the journey home took a lot longer than the one coming out as heavy lorries negotiated winding lanes ahead of them.

'Will you be back there tomorrow, Simon?' Caro's

dad asked politely.

'Yes, soon as it gets light.'

'That's dedication for you. No work then?'

'I'm still at school, St Luke's.'

'Really! So you know each other then?'

'Yes, slightly,' Caro butted in.

'I thought you were all on work experience,' Mrs McCarthy said.

'Simon's fell through – they couldn't take him in the end,' Caro blurted out.

Simon gave her an odd sidelong look and she blushed fiercely. Why did she always feel this need to interfere? So what if he'd been dismissed. What was that to her? Why did it matter if her parents realised, as they probably already did, that this was the oaf and slob she'd complained so bitterly about.

'Better luck next time, lad,' Mr McCarthy said mildly and then, thankfully, started to chat to his wife.

In the back there was a strained silence until they reached the centre of town. A little while later Simon leant forward to indicate a bus stop where he said he'd like to be dropped off. Caro didn't think it was that near to where he lived but forced her tongue to keep still. Simon appeared as glad to get out of the car as Caro felt for him to go.

'Nice lad. Very quiet though,' Mrs McCarthy observed as they pulled away from the kerb again, towards Lucy's house. Caro smiled to herself in the darkness. She wondered what the teachers would make of such a description being applied to Simon Mitchel.

Later, in bed, Caro found her thoughts wandering back to Simon. He was such an unpredictable character. When she'd decided he was a yob, he showed some redeeming qualities; when she tried to trust him, he went shoplifting. Now he was suddenly a conservationist, working all hours to save her favourite beach. Tomorrow he could be . . . anything!

'Time your light was out,' Mrs McCarthy called, passing on the landing.

'Mum!'

'What is it?'

'Come and chat.'

'Look at the time, and you've got work tomorrow.'

'Just a minute.'

Mrs McCarthy balanced her mug of coffee on the chest of drawers, gathered up some clothes strewn on the bed and made herself comfortable. Caro shifted her weight onto one elbow.

'How did you get oil on your nose?' her mum asked, dabbing at it with a finger.

'It's all over my jeans. Has Dad got some of that gunk stuff?'

'Bound to – the garage reeks of it.'

'That was Simon tonight, you know, *the* Simon.'

'We thought so. Looks better with that haircut.'

'Michael fired him.'

'What for?'

'Oh, something stupid in the end, but he'd been shop-lifting the day before. He didn't really try.'

'He deserved it, then.'

'Yes, but not everything he gets . . .'

'You like him?'

Caro glanced at her mum to see if she was teasing, but the quiet grey eyes were serious.

'Sometimes, but I also dislike him. He's all over the place. You never know what he's going to do next.'

'He's quite a serious lad.'

'*Serious*?'

'Oh yes, you can tell. He'd have to really believe in something before he could get worked up about it, but once he *was*, there'd be no stopping him. Like Green-peace. He obviously believes in that.'

'Then why not school, and work? The rest of us have to.'

'Perhaps he hasn't had the encouragement and support that you've had. School never seems very worthwhile at the time. It's usually later that you regret not making the effort.'

78

'I don't know whether he's a decent person or not. I think *one* thing, then he goes and does something totally opposite.'

Mrs McCarthy started to laugh. 'Typical Caro. Always wanting to put people in pigeon holes and make sure they stay there.'

'That's not so!' Caro protested.

'I'm afraid it is, love. You like to be right, and if people keep changing, so do your opinions of them. It can be very unsettling.'

'Well, how can you trust someone? I mean how many times do you cover for someone like Simon before you say enough's enough?'

'Perhaps you shouldn't 'cover' for him at all. If he makes mistakes he has to live with them. What you *can* do is be kind and friendly all the time. Don't judge people so quickly. It's an easy habit to acquire. We're always being told to judge by first impressions, but Jesus wasn't like that. He told us not to judge anyone or start condemning because if we did, we'd be asking to be judged ourselves. Nobody's perfect. We've all got our nasty sides or our guilty secrets. Living and getting on with people means forgiving their bad points and loving them just for what they are.'

'I wasn't ashamed of Simon this evening in the car. I just didn't want him to get embarrassed explaining why he was dismissed.'

'I know, but Simon's a big lad. He can take care of himself and he mustn't think that you're ashamed or he'll just see you as another one of the stuck-up goody goodies he so despises.'

'Oh, crikey!' Caro sighed.

'You ought to persuade him to go back to school.'

'How can *I* do anything?' Caro wailed. 'He wouldn't listen to me.'

'You could find a way, I expect,' Mrs McCarthy said, sliding gently off the bed. She kissed her daughter lightly on the forehead before flicking the bedroom light switch.

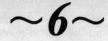

~6~

Although not everyone could manage every evening, the Youth Club provided a contingent of willing volunteers each evening for the next three days. Caro and Lucy had vowed to be there for as many sessions as it took, but they were as relieved as everyone else when, on the last evening, Peter Stride informed them that all that could be achieved by hand *had* been. From this point on, chemical detergents used at sea and a specially imported boom to contain the remaining large slick would tackle the job more effectively than handfuls of volunteers removing oily sand bucket by bucket. An important development that greatly assisted the council was the intervention by a local landowner whose estate bordered Budle Beach. It was in all the local papers that a certain member of the emergency committee had more or less insisted on the disaster fund being radically revised to allow for twice as much paid manpower and the hire of extra heavy plant.

'Money talks as usual!' Mr McCarthy had commented, browsing through the paper after supper one evening.

'Well, the fund *should* be increased,' Caro had said.

'Of course, but I'd like to think it *would* have been anyway, without all the string pulling that goes on.'

'You're just being cynical,' his wife had said, not very

convincingly. Mr McCarthy simply smiled.

'How can anyone *demand* more money being spent on the clean up?' Caro insisted, worrying away at her father like a terrier with a bone.

'Because they own land that the housing department wish to buy next year.'

'Blackmail, you mean?'

'Not exactly. It's never as blatant as that. It's just a case of "you scratch my back and I'll scratch yours". It's perfectly common practice in business circles and definitely in politics.'

'But what's in it for this landowner? He just wants to see the beach cleaned.'

'I imagine his motives aren't quite as pure as that. I believe he owns land near Budle Beach which may be granted planning permission soon. If so, the lease to build things like a cafe, leisure complex or caravan park will be affected by the state of the beach. Naturally he needs it to look its best.'

'That's really underhand,' Caro complained.

'Well, at least it's worked out for the best this time,' her father pointed out.

'And if any ordinary concerned member of the general public had wandered in and asked for special help they'd have been sent packing! I think the system stinks!'

'Perhaps you'd better get into politics, love,' Mrs McCarthy had laughed, picking up the tail end of the conversation.

'No, thank you very much.'

'It's the only way to change things. No good putting your head in the sand.'

A few days later Caro was still running through this in her mind. Having decided she wanted nothing more to do with high finance and business, Caro was still acutely aware of how much power certain people had to change situations and affect people's lives. On the other hand, good people like Pearl who worked her fingers to the bone were constantly being put upon and used by others in authority while none of her demands were listened to. Caro was torn. She wanted a job as selfless and caring as Pearl's, but she also wanted the power to make things happen.

Take the sea birds for example. As the days had gone by, despite Pearl's arguments with the RSPB and local charities, a further twenty-five victims had been more or less dropped on her doorstep. With neither the space nor the time, Sandy and Pearl were at their wits' end, but still no help was offered and the birds continued to arrive.

Caro had gone so far as to phone Mrs Clarke at school and ask if there was any way in which she could be released from Michael's salon so she could spend all day at the cats' home. Mrs Clarke had been adamant in her refusal.

'You can't mess people around, Caro, and I'm surprised you should have asked. In business you *keep* to arrangements.'

'But Pearl and Sandy *need* me this week.'

'That isn't the point, Caro. I'm sorry, but a level of commitment is what employers are looking for and I'm trying to teach you all what that means. In any case, I've heard glowing reports of you from both establishments, and you wouldn't want to jeopardise your final references, would you?'

Caro had accepted the decision, or at least she saw the sense in it, but that still didn't help Pearl. There wasn't a single person Caro could think of to turn to. All her school friends were in the same position and older people were somehow either too old or too busy to approach. She even contemplated asking her mum whether *she* could spare a few hours, but when Dad arrived home with his end of month accounts and left them sitting meaningfully on the kitchen table, Caro didn't have the heart.

It was Lucy who came up with the solution and Caro couldn't imagine why she hadn't thought of it herself.

'Simon Mitchel, of course. He's not doing anything this week, and he'd be just right for Pearl. Honest, reliable . . .' Lucy grinned.

'Well, perhaps I won't tell her *all* about him.'

'He may not want to do it, of course,' Lucy warned.

'Why ever not? He'd be perfect. He's hard-working, concerned . . . and he could do with *some* kind of reference.'

'Get on the phone and ask him then.'

It was at this point that Caro began to feel the idea hadn't been quite so brilliant after all.

'I can't.'

'Oh no, not this again! We saw him three evenings in a row, you chatted to him every time your paths crossed.'

'I did *not*!' Caro flared, incensed that Lucy should have taken so much notice of her casual and fleeting conversations.

'Well, at least you know him well enough to pick the phone up.'

'He might think I'm being pushy or trying to chat him up, for goodness sake,' Caro protested, going hot with embarrassment at the very thought.

'All right then, ask him if he can help out in the mornings while you're at the salon. He'll know you're just asking for Pearl then.'

Caro eyed her friend curiously for a moment. Work had definitely brought out a new side, much more organising, even a shade bossy! Remembering all the occasions she had been the one pushing and deciding for her friend, Caro was humbled into obedience. In fact, the phone call proved to be much simpler than breaking the news to Pearl the following afternoon.

'A boy who was sent home from *two* other work experiences?'

'I can explain, at least about the second one,' Caro offered, regretting her impulse to tell the whole truth about Simon.

'No thank you, dear. I'm up to my eyes in everything this week and the last thing I need is some young hoodlum getting up to goodness knows what whenever my back is turned.'

Caro was hurt and frankly surprised at Pearl's reaction. She was the last person Caro would have expected to jump to such a hasty conclusion without even meeting the person. It also placed Caro in the awful position of having to phone Simon back and tell him he wasn't wanted. Having assumed that Pearl would jump at the chance, Caro had even told Simon what time to turn up the next morning. What a stupid, embarrassing predicament to have got into, and all because . . . Caro tried to blame Lucy in her mind but it wouldn't stick. Of course she should have checked with Pearl first. But now what?

Caro wasn't in the habit of running to her mum, or indeed anyone, for help but this classed as a major trauma and, as such, was definitely best shared.

'Oh, Caro! Your impulsiveness is really going to get you in trouble one of these days!' Mrs McCarthy said, looking up from the accounts she was trying to enter in some logical order.

'I know, I know, but you've *got* to do something,' Caro pleaded.

'I've spent the entire day sorting your father out,' Mrs McCarthy frowned, waving a wadge of dog-eared invoices in Caro's direction, 'and now *you* start! I don't know.'

Seeing the look of abject despair on her daughter's face, Mrs McCarthy sighed and tried to regain her composure.

'Make me a cup of tea while I have a think.'

Caro scrambled to her feet. If her mum could solve this disaster, making tea every day for the next year wouldn't be too much to ask.

It took several cups of tea and the preparation of supper for Caro's mum to come up with an idea and even then she held out very little hope.

'The trouble is I don't even *know* Pearl, so what reason should she have for trusting my judgement?'

'I know, but you're an adult. She'll listen to you.'

'I wouldn't hold out too many hopes, and if this doesn't work you'll just have to phone Simon back. It was very irresponsible of you, Caro,' she added.

Caro didn't need to be reminded but she kept quiet, recognising her mum's annoyance as a response to the tricky situation she'd been put in. Caro made a mental note never to interfere with people's lives again. It was much more trouble than it was worth, however well-meaning you were being. Caro couldn't hear what her mum said on the phone. She didn't dare to hope Pearl might change her mind, but the look of quiet satisfaction on Mrs McCarthy's face ten minutes later as she took her apron down from the back door hook was enough to tell Caro that, somehow, she'd managed it.

'Mum, you're wonderful!' Caro screamed, dancing round her and making cutlery on the work surfaces rattle.

'It was nothing.'

'How did you do it?' Caro cried, laughing and jumping at the same time.

'What's all the noise about?' Mr McCarthy said, stomping his feet on the backdoor mat.

'Oh hello, Dad. Tell him, Mum.'

'Tell me what?'

'How you're taking that nice young lad, Simon, on work experience for a week, every afternoon starting tomorrow.'

'I'm what!'

Caro's smile faded. 'Mum!'

'Well, how else was I supposed to persuade Pearl that Simon was trustworthy enough to work at her place? The only thing I could do was show that *we* had faith in him. So, I said your father was going to employ him in the garage. Which he is.'

'Hang on a minute, Jen. I said I'd try to fix something up, maybe, when it's convenient. This week certainly isn't. Jack's on holiday and I'm stuck in the office doing paperwork.'

'Not *all* of it!' his wife reminded him crisply.

'Ah well, I know, but I can't organise a lad this week. It's out of the question. Anyway, whose bright idea was it?'

There was a moment's pause before Mr McCarthy's

gaze rested on his daughter's uncomfortable face.

'What on earth . . . ?'

'Caro can explain everything,' Mrs McCarthy smiled, turning her attention to the casserole bubbly idly in the oven.

'It was one of the best decisions I ever made, taking that lad on,' Pearl informed Sandy and Caro two days later.

Caro opened her mouth to point out just whose idea it was in the first place and how hard it had been to persuade Pearl to accept him, but she closed it again. Better to let Pearl think of it as *her* decision. Every time Simon's name was mentioned, Caro felt herself tense, expecting to hear some complaint or that he hadn't turned up. Waiting for her father's return each evening was even worse since, somehow, Caro had assumed a personal responsibility for Simon's behaviour. Eventually, however, Caro realised Simon was doing just fine without her worrying over him. He worked slavishly for Pearl and often volunteered to carry on through his lunchtime, so once or twice Caro saw him before he had to dash off to her dad's workshop.

'Everything OK, then?' she asked one day, as they passed each other in Pearl's untidy hallway.

'Your dad's a good bloke,' Simon said quietly, which seemed to Caro like pretty high praise. She felt pleased and on the spur of the moment found herself asking Simon if he'd like to go to a party that weekend.

'It's a sort of end of work experience celebration at a friend's house, well, Linda actually. You know her . . . in our Art class.'

'Oh yeah, her,' Simon didn't sound too keen.

'Of course, if you've got something else on,' Caro said quickly, feeling suddenly embarrassed.

'No.'

'You'll come then?'

'Yeah, OK'

'Good. Shall we meet at my house about seven? We can walk. It's not far.'

'Whatever you like,' Simon said, shrugging his shoulders.

'Saturday then.'

'Yeah, see you.'

Afterwards, Caro couldn't for the life of her imagine why she'd invited Simon. Linda had said bring a friend, but she wouldn't be expecting Simon Mitchel. He hadn't sounded that keen either, but then why should he? Linda's crowd weren't exactly his kind of people, now she came to think about it.

'He probably felt he had to,' Lucy said later that evening.

'Why?'

'Well, your dad giving him that work placement and everything.'

'Oh thanks! That makes me feel great. I was just hoping he might enjoy it and get to know some friendly Christian people out of school.'

'What difference will that make?'

'They'll see him as just a person, rather than a moody no-hoper who sits at the back of class and makes a nuisance of himself.'

'I shouldn't expect any miracles!' Lucy warned, dabbing her finger in a pot of eye-shadow and smearing it over the back of her hand.

'What are you wearing?'

'Probably jeans and my new top. What about you?'

'I wondered about a skirt.'

'Hm, really making an effort, aren't we?' Lucy murmured, looking up slyly.

'What about lending me that green silk scarf – it would just match. I want to weave it into a French plait.'

'You can't *do* French plaits.'

'No, but *you* can.'

'What a nerve. It takes hours and I'm meeting John at seven.'

'That's OK. Tell him to come here. We can all walk up together then.'

'Very cosy.'

'Oh come on, Lucy. I can't think of enough to chat about all the way to Linda's.'

'That's your problem, you invited Simon.'

'I promise we'll leave you alone to dance the night away once we get there.'

Lucy took aim with the pot of eye-shadow but changed her mind. 'I'll just borrow this then,' she smiled, pocketting it. 'You won't want this colour if you're going in green!'

Caro wasn't very interested in clothes or make-up as a rule, but she spent a lot of time ironing her black skirt and the crochet jumper her mum had managed to finish that morning. They looked good together. Varnished nails and matching lipgloss completed the effect and Lucy despite her grumbles, took special care with Caro's hair, deftly weaving in the scarf so that there was enough to tie in a luxurious bow at the end.

'There! Not bad though I say so myself,' she declared as Caro tried to look at the plait in her bedside mirror.

'Sure it's straight?'

'Positive. Hey, they're here.'

'Who?'

'Both of them. They must have met up on the way.'

'Oh, crikey.'

'Come on,' Lucy shouted over her shoulder as she thundered downstairs. Caro followed more sedately, partly on account of much higher heels than she was used to, and also because she didn't want to give Simon the wrong impression.

He stood slightly behind John, head down, hands in pockets. Caro felt a rush of disappointment. He hadn't made much effort to smarten up. His hair was ruffled and could have done with a wash. His shirt, though reasonably clean, wasn't properly ironed. The jeans had tell-tale oil smears which must have come from her father's workshop.

They set off, John and Lucy walking ahead, chattering away, while Caro and Simon followed more or less side by side, in awkward silence.

'You look smart,' Simon volunteered, giving her a quick glance sideways.

'Oh thanks.' Caro felt irritated that she'd taken all that time dressing up. He obviously thought it was overdone.

'Had a good day?' she asked after another few steps.

Simon scowled and gave a noncommittal grunt. Not for the first time Caro realised just how far apart their worlds were. A Saturday at home for Simon was probably light years away from Caro's experiences with her parents.

The silence had reached the awful point where even speaking would be an embarrassment, when it happened. The paving slabs were uneven and Caro felt a yank on her right foot, pinning her heel firmly between two slabs. Letting out a squeak of surprise, Caro wriggled her foot out of the shoe and stood barefoot on one toe trying to retrieve her shoe without ripping the heel off. Lucy and John had disappeared. Mortified and angry, Caro could have turned and run home, especially when she looked up and saw the amusement on Simon's face.

'Stupid shoes!' she mumbled, now completely humiliated.

'Sorry, let me have a go,' Simon offered bending down. 'You look like Cinderella,' he added grinning up at her.

'Very funny. Goodness knows why I wore the daft things.'

'They look nice. Just a bit useless for walking,' Simon said, finally pulling the heel free. 'Bit scratched I'm afraid.'

Caro snatched the shoe from his hand and hopped around like a sparrow as she struggled to get it back on.

'Thanks!' she muttered crossly. Once Caro had straightened her skirt and tested the now slightly wobbly heel she was able to see the funny side of the situation. At any rate it had broken the ice and as they walked on, Caro skipping the cracks strategically, there suddenly seemed plenty to chat about.

Linda's house glowed like a beacon as they rounded the corner. Lights beamed out from every window and the thud of pop music blaring from somewhere downstairs reached their ears a long time before they got inside.

Caro was surprised to see so many people, a lot of whom she didn't recognise. Linda's parents had evidently left her to it, because there were no adults hovering in the background. Linda appeared briefly as they wandered in through the front door. She laughed and waved, but looked very flushed and anxious.

'What a squeeze!' Caro gulped, as they wriggled their way into the kitchen to fetch drinks.

'I don't remember inviting quite so many people,' Linda said, her eyes flickering nervously over their heads.

'I hope you don't mind me bringing Simon,' Caro said hastily.

'Oh no, course not, it's just the others . . .' she sighed waving an arm vaguely in the direction of the lounge.

'Aren't your parents coming back?'

'I persuaded them to leave me until eleven o'clock, absolutely forbade them to come back before then.' Linda sounded as if she rather regretted her insistence on being so independent now.

'It'll be OK,' Caro said, more confidently than she felt.

'Come on, Linda!' shouted some tall boy Caro didn't know. He grabbed Linda's arm and pulled her towards the lounge where people were dancing.

'Drink?' Simon suggested.

'What is there?'

'Shandy, juice, coke . . . punch, wine,' Simon said, raising his eyebrows.

'Wine!' Caro surveyed the half-empty bottles ranged along the work surface dubiously. There was no way Linda's parents would have allowed wine. Someone must have brought it along.

'I'll just have a juice,' she said firmly, and felt very relieved when Simon poured the same for himself.

This was supposed to have been a group of her Christian friends, people who would chat to Simon and let him realise just how friendly and normal they were. Unfortunately there were far more outsiders, many of whom Caro barely knew and a few of whom she had heard plenty about, none of it good. She guessed that a great many of them had gatecrashed. With no one really in charge the situation was explosive. Caro toyed with the idea of going home right away, but then Linda looked as if she could do with some support.

'Dance?' she shouted, above the hubbub.

'Whatever,' Simon replied, shouldering his way ahead of her.

The lounge was stifling hot and smelly. What Caro could see of the floor was liberally spotted with spilled drinks and trodden in crisps. At least Linda's parents had rolled back the carpets, but they were going to be livid when they saw this mess. Dancing was difficult in such a jam, with elbows constantly jabbing in her sides and people treading on her feet. After two or three records had played, Caro pointed to the hall and began squirming her way out of the crowd.

'Its almost impossible to move, let alone dance!' she moaned, as they propped themselves against a wall in the hall and gulped in fresh air from the open door.

'Your friends' parties always like this?' Simon asked.

Caro shook her head. 'I'm sorry. It's ghastly, isn't it?'

'I don't mind. There's nothing much else to do on a Saturday night on your own.'

'Is your dad out a lot then?' Caro asked, trying not to sound surprised.

'Pretty much all the time, thankfully.'

'I'm sorry,' Caro murmured, confused.

'Why should you be sorry?'

'Well, it must be tough not getting on with your parents. I think mine are a pain sometimes but . . .'

'Crikey, Caro, you don't know you're born. If I had parents like yours, I'd be laughing.'

'Yes, I know I'm lucky.'

Raised voices from the kitchen made them both look up. This was followed by the sound of breaking glass and screams of laughter. Caro flattened herself against the wall as half a dozen people erupted out of the room.

'Where's Linda?' Lucy hissed, suddenly appearing at Caro's elbow.

'Who knows! Where have you been?'

'Dancing, or trying to. Honestly, things are getting well out of hand. They're throwing food around in there and have you tasted the punch?'

'No, I'm on juice.'

'Well, it's laced with something – half the people here are getting drunk and behaving stupidly.'

'Shall we go?'

'What about Linda and Sarah?'

'Where's Sarah?'

'Upstairs crying!'

'Oh, great.'

'Apparently someone spilled red wine down her new dress and it's ruined.'

'So what?' Caro said crossly. 'She should be down here sorting things out. Linda's mum and dad are going to go beserk. She'll be grounded for the rest of her life at this rate. Do you know her date?'

'Never seen him before.'

'Well, can't *he* do something?'

'If you ask me he's in a worse state than some of the others.'

'Someone ought to clear up that glass before anyone gets hurt,' Simon pointed out.

'Come on then,' Caro replied.

In the kitchen they searched for a dustpan and brush and began clearing up the debris. A bottle and three glasses had smashed. Caro couldn't believe that whoever was responsible had just walked off and left it. The puddle of liquid swilling in the middle of the glass made brushing it up almost impossible. Lucy took the opportunity to tip a final half-bottle of wine down the sink. It smelt cheap and vinegary. Simon was on his knees picking up the larger pieces of glass when Linda and her boyfriend burst through the door.

Seeing the state of her kitchen and Simon in the middle of it, Linda let out an anguished wail and started to cry. 'Oh, Paul!' she sobbed, 'Look at it! What's Mum going to say?'

'OK you, get on your feet,' Paul said rather thickly.

Lucy spun round, a cloth in her hand to attempt an explanation, but Paul had already advanced on Simon, grabbing him by the shirt collar. A button spurted off and spun into the wine puddle.

'What do you think you're doing, mate?' Simon growled, his hands clenching into fists.

'We know all about you, Mitchel. Do you want to leave or shall I make you?'

'You and whose army?' Simon muttered dangerously, squaring up to him.

'Simon, please,' Caro said putting a hand on his arm. He tensed but didn't shake her off.

'Hiding behind yer girlfriend, slob!' Paul sneered, swaying slightly on his feet.

'Linda, we were clearing up!' Caro said, speaking clearly and slowly to make sure the bewildered and befuddled girl understood.

'Then who . . . ?' she began, wiping her nose.

'Some of *his* friends, I shouldn't wonder,' Caro snapped, jerking her head in Paul's direction.

He scowled at her and continued to square up to Simon. 'Come on then, come on!'

'Oh wrap up, Paul,' Linda said, getting a grip on herself at last.

'What's your problem? Loosen up a bit, kid,' Paul drawled, lurching violently against the table, upsetting another bottle.

'Be careful!' Caro shouted.

'It's a party, chick, not a Sunday School outing.'

'Don't call her that,' Simon said quietly.

Paul's eyes narrowed and then he giggled nastily. 'God, what a load of wets! Should have expected it,

I suppose, getting mixed up with the God squad,' he drawled.

'I think it's time you went home,' Linda said, quite calm and cool now.

'Gonna make me, honey?' he laughed.

'No, I am,' Simon said, stepping decisively towards him.

Caro bit her lip in horror as Simon grappled with Paul, sending a chair toppling noisily to the floor. She looked up at John in appeal, but he spread his hands and stayed out of it. Paul was at least a head taller than Simon and broad-shouldered, but the drink had slowed his reflexes and Simon, clear-headed and quick, dodged his aimless punches, confusing him with nimble side-steps. Tiring quickly, Paul staggered around until he was sent down by a well-judged jab to the stomach which winded him. As he struggled up cursing, Simon grabbed his wrist, twisting the arm up his back until the boy flopped around helplessly.

'Leave off!' he yelled.

'I'll just see you to the door, mate,' Simon replied with a grim smile. The people who had gathered to watch the fray, parted before them as Simon propelled the other boy quickly down the hall and out of the door. Deflated now, Paul staggered off down the drive without a backward glance.

Simon smiled at the amazed faces in the hall before tapping his watch meaningfully. 'Party's over folks! Time to go home.'

There were one or two grumbles, but most people were prepared to pick over the pile of coats in the hall, gather their belongings and go.

Linda, looking strained and pale, came out to wave people off. Some of them avoided her eyes, others murmured apologies. Finally, there was just the blare of music, louder now without the mass of bodies absorbing the sound. Linda picked her way across the floor and switched the stereo off. Silence beat at their eardrums.

'I'm going to be dead,' Linda said, subsiding onto the

sofa as she surveyed the debris at her feet. Palls of smoke hung in the air, half-empty glasses perched precariously on every conceivable surface and the floor was sticky and wet.

'Look, thanks, Simon. Things could have got nasty without you. I'm sorry about Paul – I never knew he could be such an animal,' Linda added, her voice trembling with emotion.

Caro felt a great rush of sympathy for the girl. 'There must be something we can do,' she said brightly.

'Mum and Dad'll be here in half an hour. Look at the state of this.'

'Well, we can make it look a *bit* better,' Lucy said.

John jumped up and threw open some windows. Fresh air rushed in, cutting through the stale smoke. Karen and Caro collected glasses, crisp bowls and ash trays, while Simon straightened ornaments, picked up cushions and dragged furniture away from the walls. Encouraged by the improvement, Linda shook herself into action, dragged Sarah downstairs and began to mop the floor with hot soapy water.

'Perhaps we should dump these wine bottles?' Lucy suggested in the kitchen.

'Good idea and let's start washing up,' Caro said as she shot a mess of paper plates and half eaten sandwiches into the bin.

By the time Linda's parents' car rumbled into the drive they were still up to their arms in suds, but the overall impression was decidedly better. The adults sniffed apprehensively as they entered the hall, but Linda's mum was evidently relieved to see nothing seriously amiss and slightly surprised to find the party over.

'Everything OK, love?' Linda's dad said, popping his head round the corner.

'Yes, well, there were one or two problems. I'll tell you about them later. This lot have been great,' she added indicating the four cleaners.

'We ought to let you go, though, Have you all got lifts home?'

'It's OK. We're walking together,' John said.

Caro gave the table a final flick with the dish-cloth and made to collect her coat.

'I don't think I've met you, dear,' Linda's mum said, eyeing Simon a shade suspiciously.

'Simon's a friend of mine,' Caro interrupted, putting paid to any more questions.

The night air was still and pleasant.

'Quite a party!' Lucy observed.

'Incredible how quickly you can transform a disaster area once you get organised,' Caro added

She glanced at Simon apprehensively. What a way to introduce him to her friends! Still, he'd been great. Linda would be eternally grateful to him at any rate. Moments later he surprised her by saying, 'Not a bad evening. I quite enjoyed it actually.'

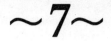

~7~

Going back to school was a strange experience for Caro. Wearing a uniform, and sliding back into the routine of days punctuated by bells, homework, assemblies and classes seemed suddenly childish. Lucy had changed too, seeming much more determined and organised. She had set her heart on nursery nursing and now spent lunch times poring over college courses and any related background reading she could lay her hands on.

Mrs Clarke organised debriefing interviews with everyone to discuss the work experience and reports from employers. Caro's dad had had to fill in a long complicated sheet detailing Simon's performance, punctuality, presentation and general skills. Mr McCarthy's honest appraisal had gone a long way to placating Mrs Clarke. She decided not to refer to Simon's misdemeanours to the Headmaster, and when Pearl's glowing references arrived she actually began to view Simon's presence in her Careers lessons with less scepticism.

'Perhaps we'll find you suitable employment yet, Simon,' she conceded.

Certainly in Careers, Simon behaved a little better, taking some interest in the different opportunities outlined and occasionally copying down an address or college course that might be useful. In every other lesson, however, his boredom was patently clear and within a week the surly scowl had returned. More than once Caro saw him slouching against a corridor wall having been thrown out of this or that lesson for disruptive or insolent behaviour. At such times she felt a mixture of disappointment and irritation. Simon could be so charming, and enthusiastic too when it suited him. This oafish response to any situation he didn't particularly enjoy frustrated her.

'What is it this time?' she demanded, catching him lingering outside the Year Head's office one lunchtime.

'The usual. Winters kicked me out,' Simon said. His shoulders were hunched and he stabbed his heel against the skirting board viciously.

'Why don't you just toe the line?' Caro demanded, exasperated.

'What's the point? I don't need Chemistry and Winters always picks on me.'

'So ignore him. Just sit there!'

Simon turned away to glance out across the playground.

Caro sighed and began to walk away, but Simon suddenly called her back.

'Hey, I was wondering if you wanted to go on a protest rally with me.'

'A protest rally?' Caro sounded dubious.

'We're protesting against the cleaning out of oil tankers off Torbay. A march to the town hall then handing over a petition. On Thursday after school.'

'Well, I don't know . . .' Caro had never been on a protest rally. Various alarm bells rang in her head.

'Forget it, then!' Simon scowled, turning his back on her again, dismissive.

Torn between her better judgement and wanting to somehow support Simon, Caro found herself agreeing to meet him on Thursday before the Year Head's door opened and Simon went in.

Caro walked off, confused, wondering how she was going to explain it to her parents or whether they might be better off not knowing at all.

'It's not a criminal activity,' Lucy pointed out, as they walked home together after school.

'Well, would you come, then?'

'Can't. It's Youth Club, isn't it? Kate has invited the St John's Ambulance man in to give us a demonstration of first aid.'

'Oh!' Caro was mortified. She'd forgotten all about it, and it was a session she particularly wanted to attend.

'Tell him you can't make it.'

'I can't,' Caro sighed.

'Crikey, it's not a date!' Lucy pointed out, adding mischievously, 'Or perhaps it is!'

'No, of course it is *not*,' Caro frowned, 'but he'll think it's a put down and go off in a sulk. You know what he's like.'

'He's not your lame duck, Caro. Look at what you've done for him already.'

'Remember who got us out of trouble at the party,' Caro reminded her, 'and anyway, I didn't *do* anything much. Simon got his own good grades on work experience.'

'Much good it'll do him. He's on detention twice already and it's only Tuesday!'

'Oh well, I said I'd go, so I'll have to. Give my apologies to Peter.'

'Will do. I'll tell him you're protesting, shouting at the Mayor, throwing bottles at the town hall!'

'Don't you dare. Anyway if it's to do with Greenpeace it'll be exactly that – peaceful – so it'll just be a quiet walk, deliver our petition and go home!'

'Nothing to worry about then,' Lucy taunted.

'No, of course not,' Caro said, much more positively than she felt.

When Thursday came Caro just couldn't bring herself to tell her parents that she was off on a rally. It wasn't that she felt there was anything really wrong about going, but she was sceptical about her parents' response. For one thing they would want to know every last detail about the rally which she didn't know herself; for another they might just forbid her to go, and then Simon would assume she'd chickened out. When Caro left the house at seven, therefore, she let her mum assume that she was on her way to church with Lucy. Afterwards, Caro promised herself, she would tell them exactly where she'd been, and when they heard how responsibly the rally had been led and organised they would be perfectly happy. A twinge of guilt about the deception worried Caro but, as she hurried towards the park where the rally was due to gather, excitement quelled any last remnants of unease. A stiff breeze flicked her hair up and billowed it behind her. Turning up the collar of her jacket, she began to jog down the road, liking the thud of her trainers on the pavements and the scratchy sound of her jeans brushing lightly together.

There was an impressive crowd at the park, mostly young, earnest-faced people in casual, rather scruffy clothes. Caro scanned the stragglers converging on the main body of people for signs of Simon's group. It was difficult to distinguish individuals from the drab crowd. Caro felt conspicuous in her bottle green jacket and mustard sweater. She also regretted bringing her shoulder bag. Every other female seemed to be brandishing a banner or slogan-daubed home-made flags. An organiser with a loud-hailer summoned the members who floated towards the central podium like filings towards a magnet. Caro held back, trying not to get sucked in before Simon found her, but it was hard to resist the tide of people moving around her.

Just as Caro was beginning to panic, Simon materialised at her side and touched her elbow gently.

'Oh, thank goodness!' Caro smiled. 'I was getting worried.'

'I saw you as soon as you arrived but I was stuck in the crowd over there. It took some time getting out. Fantastic turn out, isn't it?'

'Er, yes. Bit claustrophobic in here though,' Caro admitted, trying to avoid stepping on toes as the throng tightened around her.

The man with the loud hailer raised his hands and waited for the chatter to subside to a low murmur. He then began his speech, outlining the aims of the rally, the route of the march and the details of the petition delivering. Caro was relieved to hear the speaker reiterating the need for peaceful pressure. She still felt odd and out of place, but as the thick crocodile weaved its way out of the park and down the High Street at a ponderous pace, the chants were subdued. Passers-by, late night shoppers and a cinema queue eyed the marchers with curiosity. Some knots of youths shouted derisive comments, a few old age pensioners looked on with bewildered or disapproving shakes of the head. Most of the onlookers simply ignored them. At the South Street crossroads the marchers turned right, cutting across the traffic and bringing cars to a standstill. Caro saw the queue of motorists sighing or swearing behind their steering wheels as the line crawled by endlessly. Lights turned from red to green and back to red while the procession continued.

'Why don't we stop and let a few cars pass?' Caro said, as they approached the kerb.

Simon stared at her pityingly, 'Maximum disruption, Caro. We keep people waiting so they take note of our banners and think about our cause.'

Caro, watching the faces of the drivers, had a feeling that was the *last* thing they'd be doing.

'Is there anything to be gained by *annoying* people?' she asked tentatively.

'It's time people were *forced* to stop and take notice of US!' Simon growled. 'They're happy to spoil and abuse the world as they rush around in their cars, belching out pollution or slap on the make-up animals have had to die to produce . . .'

'Yes, I know all that,' Caro interrupted soothingly, 'but what Greenpeace needs is co-operation not *conflict*. These motorists will just go home in a filthy temper, calling us a load of crackpots. What will *that* do for your cause?'

'Are you sorry you came?' Simon asked, accusingly.

'No, I believe in what the petition stands for, but I'm just wondering what effect all this is having on the local general public.' Caro lowered her voice, aware of people around them listening in.

They reached the kerb and Caro hesitated, thoroughly embarrassed by the sharp beep of car horns impatiently sounding. Simon pulled her none too gently into the road so that the line of marchers would not be broken. Glancing up, Caro found herself eyeball to eyeball with the puce-coloured face of her neighbour, Mr Westfield. His fists were white-knuckled on the wheel and he glared in angry surprise as Caro passed his bumper. Oh, great, Caro thought, wondering whether Mr Westfield would drive straight round to her home to complain to her parents. It was just typical that of all the motorists she could have passed it *had* to be someone who knew her.

They were now in the main street and shoppers, forced to step into doorways to avoid being trampled, changed from being curious onlookers to irritable opponents. One old lady brandishing her umbrella practically beat a path through the marchers, smacking Caro painfully in the shin. As she passed, Caro caught the mumbled words, 'Young layabouts, nothing better to do', which made her flush with anger and then experience a curious twinge of embarrassment.

Simon was in his element, chanting the now familiar slogans louder and more insistently to drown out the comments from the watchers. Caro even found herself mouthing the words, partly to drown out her doubts but mostly because everyone *else* was chanting. The march progressed, faster now as the town hall came in sight. A council meeting was in progression. The police had cordoned off the entrance area and stood around idly chatting as the crowd advanced.

Well before the main doors were reached, the leaders, after a quick confab with town hall officials, were whisked down a side alley leaving the main body of protesters heaving gently before the ropes and knots of policemen. It all seemed an anti-climax. In less than half a minute the petitioners re-emerged from a shady side-door having handed over their papers and were being ushered firmly away by a large policeman.

'Is that it, then?' Caro said, a little non-plussed.

'No way! We're staying here until they move us!' a rough-looking combat-jacketed youth declared, jostling against Caro's elbow.

She ignored him and turned to Simon questioningly.

'Well, we hang around a while, just to make our point. They'll hear us chanting from inside,' Simon said.

'And be all the more likely to read and take note of our petition!' Caro replied, heavily sarcastic.

'If people won't make reasonable decisions when they're asked, you have to *demand*,' Simon said.

Caro was torn. She deeply sympathised with the demands in the petition and was at one with the aims of Greenpeace, but she had severe doubts about the effectiveness of this kind of protest. Had it comprised white-collar workers, office workers, mums, dads and children, perhaps the impact might have been different, but gazing around she saw a mass of figures most of whom the authorities would lump together as troublemakers, just as she had classed Simon from her initial impressions. Yet they *weren't* troublemakers. Most of them were good, decent, concerned young men and women who wanted the world to be a better, safer, healthier place. Caro watched the policemen, a wall of dark uniforms, and felt sorry for them. She wondered what opinions they held. It didn't matter either way for they had a job to do. They weren't allowed to express an opinion. Behind them, town hall officials in dark suits looked testily at the seething crowd. They had a job to do, too, and this ungainly, noisy rabble was just an irritation.

'We could be protesting about the price of bread for all they care,' Caro announced flatly.

'Don't be such a defeatist,' Simon replied.

'I'm not! I'm just thinking there could be better ways of making your point than this!'

'Suggest one,' Simon challenged.

'I don't know exactly but I'm sure this isn't doing it.'

'Why?'

'Look at us! We're in the way, a noisy rabble getting on everyone's nerves. The next time anyone sees a Greenpeace slogan they'll remember *us*. Hours spent clogged in a traffic jam. Time wasted as they tried to do their late night shopping!'

'Well, they ought to be inconvenienced,' Simon spat out the words in frustration. 'Perhaps then they'll take notice.'

'Or become even more resistant!'

'How do you work that out?'

'OK. Remember being hauled into the Year Head's office?'

'So?'

'What happened?'

'He kept me kicking my heels all lunch time.'

'And then . . .'

'Wittered on about what the school expects . . . I don't see the point.'

'What did *you* do?'

'Bunked off the rest of the afternoon.'

'So his "inconveniencing" you didn't work much, *did* it?' Caro pointed out meaningfully.

Simon squirmed uncomfortably under her accusing stare.

'This is different.'

'No, it isn't! They don't want to listen, so we chant at them like a mob of deranged loonies. Result? They listen even less. Which is precisely how *you* react at school.'

'So you reckon this is all a waste of time.'

'A lot of it, *yes*,' Caro said.

'And in that case we're all totally powerless,' Simon scoffed.

'No, but we have to think of more effective ways of

getting our ideas across. People will listen to what affects *them* or their children. Everyone's interested in green issues these days, but I'm also pretty sure they're sick and tired of being nagged and shouted at. Life's hectic enough without more stresses and strains being put on them. Dad says . . .' Caro stopped, afraid of the odd glances she was getting from immediate neighbours, afraid too of sounding prissy.

'Go on,' Simon said. 'I'm listening to your alternative world-shattering ideas.'

Caro ignored the ridicule and battled on. 'Dad says the way to make people change their minds is to give them a good reason, a personal reason, why they'd be better off if they did.'

'The whole world would be better off listening to Greenpeace,' Simon said.

'You know that and so do I, but at the moment the message is all negative. A list of what they *can't* do. Naturally no one's interested. Now, some information about things they *can* do or the benefits that apply individually to them would be much more likely to get their attention.'

'But some things they'll just have to sacrifice.'

'Of course, but there are two sides. You can look after the world and still enjoy it, surely.'

'Yes, no one's arguing about that.'

'I'm just saying let's not alienate the people out there,' Caro said, waving her arm at the public passing them by, 'who *could* be on our side. We don't need them on marches, we need them changing their attitudes.'

Simon regarded her silently, thoughtfully. 'That's some speech,' he said at last.

Caro dropped her gaze, embarrassed that he should be taking the mickey out of her. 'All right what do *I* know. Maybe this *is* effective.'

'I wasn't laughing,' Simon said. 'Do you want to go home?'

'No, I'll stay here. It looks like we're moving.'

In response to the loud hailer, the crowd did an about

turn and marched away, back to the park via the shortest route through precincts and arcades. Caro was worried for a moment that some of the more rowdy elements who had become dangerously restive during the long stationary wait might suddenly explode, but as the chanting subsided so did the electricity in the atmosphere. A series of speeches in the park, difficult to follow through the distortions of the hailers, rounded off the evening. Caro and Simon were among the first to wriggle their way out of the crowd and break away.

It was a relief to feel like an individual again, without strange hands and knees prodding you. Caro felt hot and crumpled despite the sharpness of the air. She looked at her watch. It was just before half past eight.

'Do you want me to walk you home?' Simon offered, gallantly for him.

Caro smiled mischievously. 'Actually, I was thinking of popping into the church Youth Club for the last hour. Fancy coming?'

'Do I have a choice?'

'Of course you do, but . . .'

'But you came with me so . . .'

Caro laughed. 'I wouldn't do that to you. Come along if you want, otherwise I'll see you around.'

Simon looked as if he'd much rather avoid the Youth Club, but he reluctantly agreed and they set off through the darkening streets.

When they arrived the first aid demonstration was over and the invited guests were packing up. Caro and Simon slipped in quietly and joined Lucy and several others drinking coffee in the Strides' huge basement lounge. All the furniture was tatty but comfortable, and Caro sank into an armchair thankfully. Simon hesitated before joining her on a neighbouring sofa.

'I feel a bit out of place here,' he whispered, sipping coffee nervously.

'No more than I did at that rally!' Caro returned crisply.

'What do you mean?'

'Well, I felt overdressed for a start, and some of them obviously thought so too from the looks I got.'

'You just have to ignore it, don't you.'

'Exactly!' Caro returned. 'So just relax. Everybody's friendly here.'

'Yeah, but I'm not one of you, am I?'

'I'm not a paid up member of Greenpeace either.'

'That's a bit different though.'

'How?'

'Well, anyone can be a member of Greenpeace, can't they?'

'And anyone can be a member of God's family. You don't have to know all there is to know or be one hundred per cent certain of all the issues. Hardly anyone is. You can't disagree with the basic ideas of Christianity – after all, most of the laws of the modern world are based on it. Just like Christians wouldn't disagree with what Greenpeace and organisations like it stand for.'

'The trouble with most Christians I've ever met is that they don't *do* anything about other peoples' concerns.'

'That's not true!' Caro protested hotly. 'You're just tarring everyone with the same brush. It's like me saying that all protesters just go along for the shouting and aggro – they don't *do* anything.'

'There's a few people, I'll admit, who let the organisation down by their stupid actions, but most people in Greenpeace work darn hard and don't get paid a penny for it. There are volunteers who go out clearing canal banks and marshes every weekend just for the love of it. No one even knows it's going on.'

'And there are Christians who actively support charities that *you* don't know about either! The trouble with any organisation is that it becomes associated with all its members' actions – the good and the bad. Only it's usually the bad that sticks. But it's not fair to assume that all Christians are self-satisfied, self-righteous people who sit at home in their comfortable houses doing nothing.'

'And it's not fair to assume that all Greenpeace members are lefty freaks who are anti every kind of authority,' Simon countered.

Caro sighed, accepting the criticism of his reply. He was right. She didn't like his judgement about Christians, but she was a bit too ready to act in the same way about *his* colleagues.

'Agreed. Can we call a truce?' she offered.

Simon swilled his coffee and the sparks died in his eyes. He smiled and relaxed back in the sofa. 'Truce,' he said.

They were distracted by a general rearrangement of furniture happening around them.

'What now?' Simon asked.

'Bible study,' Caro said, expecting some derogatory response. Actually she didn't care. Caro was beginning to accept that some people would laugh at her faith and try to pick holes in it. It was pointless trying to pretend that you didn't care or avoiding the subject altogether. A year ago, Caro would have felt acutely embarrassed now, afraid of Peter Stride sounding soppy or over the top, and of Simon poking fun at her or at the whole thing. What she was beginning to realise was that God didn't need too much defending. His message was open to everyone and it was their choice whether to accept it or dismiss it. God used his people to introduce others to him, and if you did your honest best to live up to that responsibility, no more could be asked. If Simon went home completely unmoved by the experience of meeting Christians and hearing a part of their faith, it didn't matter. Who knew what tiny seed had been scattered and when it might grow to produce an amazing harvest?

The Bible study actually gave Caro a lot to think about herself, so she was hardly aware of Simon's response as they heard the reading about the Good Samaritan. Peter invariably found a way of making a very familiar passage come to life by looking at it from a different angle. This evening he pointed out that the poor, attacked victim was not helped by the people he could have expected to show pity, but by the alien who had no reason to show mercy and nothing to gain by doing so.

Caro found herself smiling as they discussed the passage. If Simon was listening he would be surprised to find that his criticism of Christians not *doing* anything was shared by Jesus as he had told this story. It made her think of other things, however, like the cleaning-up operation. For those few evenings the whole community had worked together to save the beach and the wildlife. It hadn't mattered then whether you were a paid council worker, a wealthy landowner, a Christian or a member of the RSPB. The point was that there was a job to do and everyone threw their weight behind it. It was just a pity that, once the immediate crisis was over, everyone went back to their 'sides' and started arguing with or plotting against everyone else. The council meeting inside the town hall, the Greenpeace members outside it. Yet surely it was possible to compromise on *some* things – to find a way of working with other groups all the time, for everyone's good?

The evening was drawing to a close. Peter Stride shook Simon's hand and spent several minutes chatting to him. Simon seemed surprised that he remembered his name and where they had met. His gentle, but powerful, presence seemed to affect Simon who found himself talking quite freely to this almost total stranger about his home life, his hobbies, his disastrous school career, even his hopes for the future. Peter listened sympathetically, not saying much but appearing to understand everything, even what was left unmentioned. He didn't start lecturing Simon about his behaviour or attitude, but he asked a few searching questions that seemed to stop Simon in his tracks. At any rate, as they started to make their way home Simon was thoughtful and not really attentive to Caro's comments and idle chatter. They parted at the end of her road.

'Will you be all right?' Simon said, shaking himself out of his daydream.

'Yes, it's only a stone's throw. See you at school tomorrow?'

'Maybe.'

'What do you mean?' Caro asked, probing his features in the light of a street lamp for clues.

'I might bunk off.'

'Oh *Simon*!' Caro said, exasperated. 'I thought you were going to *try* this term.'

'I have done. It's no use. Nothing changes. It's still the same old drag, the same teachers hacking me off. I'm never going to get anything out of school, so why bother?'

'Well, if you're going to take that attitude, you *won't*,' Caro said, wishing she didn't sound quite so school mistressy herself.

'It's not just school, it's everything,' Simon moaned dispiritedly. 'I sometimes wonder if anything makes much difference in the end.'

'But you don't feel like that about Greenpeace,' Caro exclaimed, trying to jolt him out of this depression. 'Look at what we achieved at Budle Beach.'

'But our petition isn't going to work – *you* know it and I know it. No one will listen, and the boats will carry on flushing their tanks and there'll be another Budle Beach.'

'Don't be like that,' Caro pleaded, afraid of his cynicism.

'You said it yourself. Protest marches don't change people's minds.'

'Yes, they *do*. They might,' Caro said, clutching at straws now.

'You might as well stick to your prayers,' he concluded gloomily, and his tone suggested that this was equally futile. Caro didn't react. He was fed up. Well, she knew how that felt and as far as Simon could see, her answer to the world's problems, which was going to a Bible study, was as ineffective as his, which was to go on a protest rally.

They parted awkwardly, Simon contemplating the empty house he was about to return to, and Caro acutely aware that she had failed him and didn't have any of the

110

answers he was looking for. She couldn't wave a Christian wand and make his home life better, neither could she sway the council decision with a desperate prayer.

'Please be at school tomorrow,' Caro said as they parted.

'It doesn't make any odds whether I am or not.'

'Yes, it does, to *me*,' Caro insisted helplessly.

'I'll see,' Simon responded vaguely.

'Thanks,' Caro called, as he turned to go.

'What for?'

'This evening. It was interesting.'

Simon gave her a half smile.

'I hope you didn't mind coming to the Youth Club.'

'No, it was . . . interesting.' Simon echoed. He could have been taking the mickey, but somehow she didn't think so. She watched his slight dark figure until it turned the corner before setting off for her own door.

'Hello!' Mr McCarthy said as Caro let herself in the front door. His expression convinced Caro that Mr Westfield had already paid a neighbourly visit. 'I thought you might still be chained to a fence somewhere,' her father said, his voice heavy with disapproval.

'That was Greenham Common, Dad. Marchers don't do that any more.'

'Well, you'd *know*, wouldn't you?'

'Dad, before you start, I *did* go to church, and would you like to hear about the march from me or are you just going to assume I've been throwing bricks through windows?'

Mr McCarthy's expression softened. Relief was almost visible on his face. Caro nestled her head into his shoulder and gave him a hug. Caro knew she was going to get a lecture, but for once she was wise enough to recognise it for genuine love and concern. The fact that Simon wouldn't even have anyone at home to question him about his whereabouts seemed a lot harder to cope with.

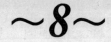

~8~

It was late when Caro finally climbed into bed, her ears still ringing from the verbal beating they'd received, mostly from her mum. The lecture had begun somewhere along the lines of trust and honesty, touched lightly on relations with neighbours – though there was general agreement that Mr Westfield *was* a busybody – and ended with the dangers of not being where you were supposed to be.

Mr McCarthy clearly felt that protest marches were a complete and utter waste of time and energy, a view which Caro had thought she shared, but she was still smarting under Simon's recriminations about Christians never *doing* anything, so she defended her decision to get involved with considerable warmth. It was her mum who finally put an end to the debate by shooing Caro upstairs and flicking light switches off in the kind of way that didn't brook any further argument.

'I haven't had any supper!' Caro had moaned from the landing.

'Too late – get undressed *now*!' her mum replied.

In bed, Caro found her mind racing with activity, thoughts buzzing around like noisy bluebottles and sleep a thousand miles away. Sighing heavily, she fought with her duvet and tried to unscramble her ideas. A shaft of light cut the blackness in two as Mrs McCarthy came into the room on padded feet. Caro smelt hot chocolate.

'Hm, thanks, Mum,' she murmured, raising herself on one elbow.

'Drink it quickly and go to sleep.'

'I can't sleep.'

'You haven't tried!'

'Just sit and talk to me for a minute, please.'

'Oh all right, but I don't want to hear another thing about marches. Once you and your dad get started there's no stopping you! It gives me a headache.'

'Actually I half agree with him,' Caro grinned in the dim light. 'But it's the principle of the thing.'

'What principle?'

'*Doing* something. Do you remember that talk we went to at church about inner city areas?'

'Oh yes, weeks ago.'

'Well, what have we *done* about it?'

'Your dad was going to get in touch with the placement scheme . . . where did he put those papers?'

'Exactly!' Caro said, pushing her point home with a loud sniff.

'He probably forgot in the process of having Simon,' Mrs McCarthy defended her husband.

'The point is, Simon's right about having to get involved with groups who start demanding things and kicking up a fuss.'

'Is that why you went – to kick up a fuss?'

'No, it's not really my scene. In fact I still think it's a waste of time, but . . . what have I got to offer that's any better?'

'Your faith,' Mrs McCarthy answered simply.

'Faith about what, Mum? That everything's going to be OK if we just leave it up to God?'

'No.'

'What then? Praying that things will change?'

'Prayer is vital. I thought you believed that.'

'I do, sort of,' Caro struggled, 'but it doesn't seem enough sometimes.'

'Prayer is a starting point, a strong tool, which leads to the correct actions and words, if we let it.'

'That's what I want to know about,' Caro said, crossing her legs under the duvet and hugging her knees tightly. 'The trouble with me is I decide what's best to do, and then end up praying that it'll all turn out OK in the end.'

'Like organising Pearl into giving Simon a placement? Yes, I remember that!'

'But it wasn't God who made that happen was it, it was *you* in the end. That's the thing I mean. Would it have all worked out just the same *without* any prayer at all?'

'Ah, that's what people *always* say, isn't it? "Perhaps it would have happened anyway." It's one of those riddles you can't ever solve. Faith isn't like that, Caro. There aren't hard and fast rules or proof positive answers. Otherwise it wouldn't be faith, would it? But without believing in God, a lot of Christians wouldn't have the courage to hope, to ask and, most especially, to find the guts to go out and *do* anything at all.'

'So God makes me bossy!' Caro laughed.

'In a way I suppose, but I think sometimes he'd rather have you listen a bit more before you rush off to have your say.'

'I know, but it's hard to wait, especially when you want things to happen.'

'First of all, make sure they are the things that *God* wants to happen,' Mrs McCarthy warned, leaning over to kiss her daughter's cheek. 'Now go to sleep!'

'Night, Mum.' Caro yawned as she snuggled down. In the soft darkness she tried to listen to God, willing herself to hear that 'still small voice' that the Bible talked about. It was hard. Suddenly her own thoughts and ideas would spring up and start babbling on, clamouring at her brain. Then, when those had been pushed aside, she would find herself day-dreaming. Annoyed, Caro sat up and pressed her fingers together tightly in an effort to concentrate. Like a small child, she began to recite the Lord's prayer, quietly and slowly. It was a funny thing, but using those familiar words calmed her more than anything else. As Caro repeated the words, 'Thy will be done', all the buzzing plans melted away and by the end of the prayer her mind was clear. Everything seemed much simpler. There were small but important things she could do as a Christian to show that she cared about her world, and about people like Simon. It wasn't necessary to shake people by the ears to make them listen. All that mattered was that she did her bit and didn't waver. As Caro slid into sleep she felt as light and carefree as a feather.

'Where is Simon Mitchel?' Mrs Clarke asked, peering around the classroom impatiently. There was silence until Tony Simpkin put up a hand tentatively.

'Well, have you see him?'

'The police came round his house this morning. He lives just up the road from me. We saw them arrive and . . .'

'Oh, right well, perhaps we'd better get on,' Mrs Clarke interrupted quickly, as two dozen curious ears pricked up. She shuffled papers noisily and began distributing them in a businesslike way which put paid to gossip. Lucy raised an eyebrow at Caro who could only shrug, mystified. As she pored over the worksheet, however, Caro could feel her heart pounding uncomfortably against her ribcage. What on earth had he done now? Remembering his odd mood of the previous evening, Caro found herself imagining the worst. Had he left her to go off on some vandalising spree or got into a fight? He surely wouldn't have gone back to the town hall to kick up a fuss.

When Caro shared these fears with Lucy at break-time, her friend couldn't help laughing. 'Crikey, Caro, you really think the best of people, don't you!'

'Well, why else do the police turn up at your door in the morning. He *must* be in trouble.'

'There could be a perfectly innocent explanation. Nobody knows here anyway, not even the teachers because Sharon overheard Mrs Clarke asking Mr Tedbury and he said no one had been in touch with the school.'

'I bet the teachers all think he's in trouble,' Caro grumbled, ignoring the fact that she had just expressed the same opinion.

'You're like a mother hen with that guy,' Lucy sighed.

'I'm just curious,' Caro lied, trying to sound casual and off-hand. 'I don't care what's happened to him,' she added, ignoring Lucy's disbelieving smile.

After school the girls had a netball match against St Maywell's school in town. Mrs Jones the PE teacher, took them down in the mini bus. The game, which they lost pretty convincingly, ended at six o'clock and the two friends opted to walk from St Maywell's which was nearer home than their own school.

'Not our best performance,' Lucy remarked, as they wandered through the chilly streets disconsolately.

'I wasn't on form,' Caro admitted. 'Mind you, did you see their goalkeeper? She was built like an Amazon. Get under her feet and you'd be crippled for life.'

'I've never seen Mrs Jones look so glad to hear the final whistle.'

'They were all over us at the end. Are you hungry?' Caro added, suddenly aware of her griping stomach.

'Absolutely starving. Fancy some chips?'

'Hm!' Caro looked up and spotted Jack's fish bar across the street.

'Come on, my treat. I've got some dinner money left over,' Lucy said, breaking into a jog.

They waited in the clammy warmth of the fish shop with mouths watering. Remembering the last time she'd been in the shop, Caro found herself looking over her shoulder, half expecting Simon to come in at any moment. Jack served suppers methodically, flipping out cod and shovelling chips with practised ease. At last they reached the head of the queue.

'Two chips, please,' Lucy said, pushing a £1 coin over the counter.

Jack dusted the bags of chips liberally with salt and drenched them with vinegar.

'Excuse me,' Caro heard herself say as she reached for the parcel. 'Have you seen Simon around lately?'

'Are you friends of his?' Jack asked, staring hard at them from under bushy white eyebrows.

'Yes, sort of,' Caro gulped weakly.

'It's a damn shame!' Jack growled, throwing a shovelful of chips into the frier with more energy than was needed.

'Where is he?' Lucy asked.

'They've taken him away.'

'The police?' Caro said.

'No, them social workers. Took off to a children's home, that's all! He didn't want to go, I'm telling you.'

Caro tried to take in this unexpected piece of information and make some sense of it. 'We heard the *police* came,' she said, in case Jack had somehow got the wrong end of the stick.

'To take his old man away, yes. Then they sent the social workers. He came here, you see. Wanted to know where he could go, but I said, "Simon, it's no good, son. They'll find you whatever." '

'*Which* children's home?' Caro insisted.

'Blackheath.'

'Is his dad ill?' Lucy asked.

'Ill in the head!' Jack shouted, tapping his forehead meaningfully. 'Always knocking him around he was. Well he went too far this time. Neighbours called the police and when they saw the state of the place, that was it.'

'He'd been hitting Simon?' Caro said, struggling to understand.

'For years. Ever since Simon's mum left home.'

'I never realised,' Caro said mournfully. How could she have spent so much time talking to Simon and never got the slightest hint that things were so bad at home. The customers in the queue behind stamped their feet impatiently.

'Thanks!' Lucy said and bundled Caro out of the shop.

They walked in silence for several hundred yards, Caro's chips congealing greasily in her unopened packet.

'What will you do?' Lucy asked at last.

'Do? It's none of my business is it?'

'You'll go and see him though,' Lucy insisted.

'I've got nothing to say to him,' Caro murmured, 'I mean, nothing to help.'

'Perhaps he'll be back at school tomorrow,' Lucy suggested. 'They'll want to get him back to a normal routine as soon as possible.'

'That's not school, then, is it?' Caro commented drily.

'Poor Simon!' Lucy whistled. 'It all happens to some people, doesn't it?'

'If only there was something we could *do*,' Caro said knitting her brows in thought.

'Let's go and *see* him,' Lucy said decisively. 'He'll be feeling pretty low, surrounded by strangers and a lot of younger kids. Come on, it's only seven, and we're less than a mile away from the place.'

'Do they let visitors in?'

'It's not a prison, Caro. Look there's a phone box. Give your mum a ring, then she can phone mine.'

Caro let Lucy drag her into the phone box and within five minutes they were on their way to Blackheath Children's Unit.

Never having been inside, the girls were pleasantly surprised at the large house set back from the road in sprawling grounds full of shrubs and trees. The front porch had stained mosaic-patterned glass in every window making it sparkle like a Christmas tree in the low late evening sunlight. A young man in jeans with designer stubble let them in and directed them to the TV lounge. Everything seemed very laid back and relaxed. Perhaps a bit too relaxed, Caro couldn't help thinking.

The helpers were all young; nobody looked like a parent or the kind of large homely figure Caro associated with such a place, someone like Pearl, for example. Lucy was ahead of her and spotted Simon first. He was spraw-

118

led on a sofa in front of the huge TV with about half a dozen kids ranging from around eleven to sixteen. His eyes were glazed and his arms folded like clamps across his grubby T-shirt.

'Hi there!' Lucy said, striding through the doorway.

Caro blushed as several pairs of eyes glared at her suspiciously. She wished they hadn't come. Simon looked like a caged animal and she felt like a spectator at the zoo.

'What you here for?' Simon grunted uncivilly.

'To see you,' Lucy replied, flopping down next to him. 'And we're whacked so don't give us a hard time. Sorry about your dad and things. This doesn't look too bad. Food OK?'

'Haven't tried it,' Simon scowled.

'Back at school tomorrow?'

'Ask *them*!' he snarled, shooting a look at the young man who had let them in as he passed the doorway.

Lucy settled back and started watching the TV. Caro couldn't believe it. Lucy was being so brutal. Deciding to try the sensitive approach, Caro sat gently next to Simon and gave him a pitying look.

'I'm terribly sorry about everything,' she said in her most soothing tone.

'Get lost!' Simon dismissed her, twisting his body into a tighter coil.

'Charming!'

'Well, don't come in here on one of your charity visits. I didn't ask to be here and I certainly don't need pains in the neck like you around, feeling sorry for me.'

'That's OK then because *I don't*!' Caro flared.

'Why are you here then?' he sneered. 'Come to say another prayer over me? Well, don't bother. This is what real life's all about. Getting shoved in a kid's home because nobody gives a toss what happens to you. Don't talk to me about being part of a big happy family and God loving everyone. There's a hell of a lot of people who could tell you different. I should know, I'm one of them.'

119

With that little tirade over, Simon jumped up and switched channels. A series of disgruntled murmurs echoed around the room, but Simon was the biggest there and his stance defied any objection.

'Would you like us to go?' Lucy said, a shade of sarcasm in her tone.

'I don't care,' Simon replied.

Caro's anger subsided as quickly as it had fired. Of course he was upset and angry. Who wouldn't be? They shouldn't have come. It was too soon. Why should he feel grateful about anything? She would have been howling her eyes out. Any parent, even a bad one, was better than no parent.

'Things *will* be OK,' she whispered.

'No, they'll probably get worse. I haven't got anything now,' Simon said, his voice flat and final.

'Can't we do something, anything?' Caro pleaded.

Simon turned on her with a twisted smile. 'Oh yes, what about a new dad, a house, a decent job. Think you can conjure those up with a quick prayer?' he scoffed.

Caro got to her feet, her lips a thin line. Biting back a few choice words of abuse she said a frosty goodbye and walked out. Lucy punched Simon on the arm lightly before following her.

'I could punch him in the mouth sometimes,' Caro screamed, as she scurried down the main path.

'Still, he was pleased we came, you could tell.'

'Are you going crazy?' Caro spun round, hardly believing her ears. 'We were about as welcome as a dose of flu.'

'Rubbish, he's got to keep up his image so he turned on us, but he was chuffed we'd bothered.'

Caro shook her head sadly. 'You're gone in the head, Lucy Baker!'

'Trust me. I've been reading up on child psychology. Shouting at you was just a release of tension. He'll be feeling tons better now.'

'Oh good!' Caro said spitefully. 'I'd like to release some tension straight on his nose.'

'*That* would be quite different,' Lucy said knowledgeably.

'Well, I'm glad it was *your* idea.'

'So am I. The thing is, what now?'

'We avoid the miserable swine and pray he changes school,' Caro suggested.

Lucy ignored her, head down, deep in thought. 'This is a challenge to our faith, Caro.'

'What do you mean?'

'Simon is asking us for help.'

'I didn't hear him.'

'All that about God . . .'

'Dismissing Christianity completely.'

'No, he wasn't. Simon is desperately trying to believe in something. He threw down the gauntlet this evening. If we don't pick it up then he really will turn his back on God, but if we let God show us what to do this could be a turning point.'

'He's right, though. We can't conjure up a new dad.'

'Of course not. God's not a fairy godmother. This is the real world we're in, but little miracles happen every day. Simon needs one tonight. We've got to go home and pray, I mean really pray. Tomorrow, *we act.*'

The two friends didn't meet again until breaktime next day when Lucy joined Caro in the school library.

'Well?' Caro asked as Lucy dumped her bag onto the table, scattering papers widespread.

Lucy looked a little flustered. 'Give me time to think. I suddenly remembered our humanities project is due in.'

'When?' Caro said, startled. How could she have forgotten.

'Next week. I haven't even started.'

'Oh crikey, I've only got a few leaflets on Rivers and Sewage.'

'Sounds lovely,' Lucy sniffed.

'It was the best I could think of. I wanted to do Pollution but all the books had gone. I got stuck with Sewage. What are other people doing?'

'Linda is working with Stewart on Fish Farming.'

'Can you work together?'

'So long as everyone pulls their weight.'

'Hey, why don't we do a joint project then, ask for an extension?'

'What on?'

'Beach pollution. I've got all the Greenpeace leaflets Simon was giving out in town.'

'What's he doing then?

'Nothing. Well, he missed most of the lessons. Have you seen him today?'

'Nope.'

'Well, that's it then. We'll see Mr King now, give him our title and get cracking at lunch time.'

'Using Simon's stuff?'

'He won't mind,' Caro assured her. 'He isn't likely to need them himself, is he?'

'Hey, that's an idea!'

'What is?' Caro asked, aware that Lucy was going off on a tangent again.

'We'll work as a three.'

'I beg your pardon?'

'We'll tell Mr King that Simon's with us. After all, he's collected all our research. We just have to write the essay, conduct a few of our own surveys, that sort of thing.'

'Is this part of your "help Simon out" plan?' Caro said dubiously.

'Not exactly, but now you mention it, everything fits in. We can go and see Simon tonight and give him the essay plan. He can be doing it while he's off school.'

'I bet he'll thank you for that,' Caro commented.

'I had a long thought about Simon last night, and then it came to me. All this time you've been thinking we have to do things *for* him. Well, I reckon he has to do things for himself. That's the only way he'll feel good about anything. He's never asked for pity. He likes people who stand up and *do* things. So we have to help him do things for himself.'

'By giving him homework?' Caro sounded highly sceptical.

'It's not just school stuff though. If he's keen on Greenpeace he'll have to learn about the real issues, won't he? The surveys we do can help Greenpeace if we do them properly. Our interviews might change people's minds, if the questionnaires are really well constructed and make people *think* for a change.'

'You could be right, I suppose,' Caro said, the grains of enthusiasm stirring in her mind.

It was during lunchtime that Caro came across some research that caught her eye. The package explored some common household goods like detergents and shampoos. A lot of them were very environmentally unfriendly, and several had their origins from the petro-chemical industry.

'Hey look, I recognise that label!' Caro explained, stabbing her finger at a page in a book they were skimming.

'Vellina vegetable-based skin and hair products,' Lucy read out. 'So?'

'Michael's salon uses them.'

'That's good, then. They're very "friendly" products. Unlike Michael!'

'I wonder . . .'

'What?'

'You remember I asked Michael about supporting the Cats' League and he said it didn't fit with his image?'

'Oh yes, you did mention it.'

'Well, he's actually supporting Greenpeace without realising it.'

'Why *does* he use the Vellina range?'

'He likes it! As simple as that.'

'What's your idea?'

'I could get him to use the fact that his salon uses Vellina to promote green issues, you know, make it part of his advertising campaign.'

'And in the process support Greenpeace,' Lucy grinned, cottoning on quickly.

'Before you know it, every salon in town will be

switching to a Vellina-type range just to compete.'

'Will Michael agree?'

'Why not? All he has to do is tell everyone how environmentally conscious he's being, while he keeps us all looking beautiful. It's a winner. He couldn't resist it. Why on earth didn't I think of it before?' Caro said, frustrated at her own stupidity.

'Get on the phone! If he says yes, we can interview him as part of the project.'

Caro was staggered at how easily Michael was persuaded. He'd willingly agreed to be interviewed even before Caro had explained about the project and what stance they intended to take. As soon as Michael realised that he was failing to exploit a part of his business that might appeal to a significant chunk of his future clients, Caro knew her idea would be snapped up.

'And I thought you'd had your fill of big business wheeler-dealing!' Lucy grinned as Caro put down the phone, her face glowing with success.

'I've changed my tack,' she replied. 'Business is fine if you make it work for the good, rather than the bad! And I've just had another idea!'

'Two in one day, careful!' Lucy said, wagging her finger gravely.

'It involves Pearl. Can you come across with me after school?'

'I suppose so. What are you going to talk *her* into?'

'Nothing much,' Caro laughed, her eyes sparkling mischievously.

Pearl was so pleased to see Caro and so welcoming to Lucy, whom she had never met, that Caro felt ashamed to have neglected her for so long. There were only a few convalescing gulls left, but more cats had arrived since Caro's last afternoon at the Sanctuary and both Pearl and Sandy looked rushed off their feet.

'Can we give a hand?' Lucy immediately volunteered, but Pearl refused firmly.

'You're all dressed in clean uniforms. I can't have you

124

getting messed up. No, you sit and have some tea with me and tell me all your news.'

'There isn't much to tell now we're back at school,' Caro said, pushing Wilkins and Spot off the table so that Pearl could lay out cups and saucers.

'And how's that nice Simon?' Pearl cooed, scrabbling in a cupboard for biscuits.

'It's partly about Simon that we came to see you,' Caro explained, as she told Pearl about Simon's predicament.

Pearl listened sympathetically but didn't seem very surprised or particularly worried that Simon had been taken away from home.

'It'll be all for the best in the end,' she commented when Caro had finished.

'But he hates it so,' Caro said.

'Of course! He's a bit of a wild thing himself when all's said and done. Having to eat regularly, wash properly and tell people where you're going will come as a bit of a shock to the lad, but if they can hold on to him for a while he might be all the better for it.'

'I was wondering,' Caro began, 'whether you could phone up Blackheath and persuade them to let Simon work here sometimes. I know he'd like it.'

Pearl nodded her head vigorously, her double chin wobbling. 'Yes, of course, if he wanted to come over at the weekends Sandy and I could always do with a hand.'

'I'd love to come too, if you'll have me,' Caro added, trying to work out where she could grab a few spare hours between homework, church and the various family outings or lazy hours she so enjoyed. It was only a matter of discipline and organisation, she decided, remembering some of the weekends she had simply wasted.

'Give Simon my love when you see him,' Pearl said, sipping her tea thoughtfully.

'We thought of going round tonight,' Lucy piped up, 'but Caro thinks we'd better leave it.'

'He's so fed up,' Caro explained, 'he gets really snappy and takes it out on me!'

'The trouble with you is that you always want to make

things perfect, when most of the time just bearable is the best we can hope for. Funnily enough, I had a call from Blackheath last week. They wanted a couple of cats.'

'Cats? What for?'

'The children. It's some new scheme they're trying to introduce. Apparently they think having some domestic pets around could help some of the younger kiddies settle. I wasn't too impressed. Very few of the staff stay for more than a year or two at the most and children move out to foster homes all the time. I felt any cats I offered could end up in a very haphazard existence with no one taking full responsibility.'

Caro understood Pearl's argument completely, but remembering the impersonal interior of Blackheath and its large high-ceilinged rooms she couldn't help but think that one or two cats mooching around would be a real improvement. Caro wondered whether to say as much to Pearl but decided against it. One favour was enough to expect. In any case, Pearl seemed preoccupied. Caro nudged Lucy and signalled for her to drink and get going. They didn't want to outstay their welcome.

'Thanks for the tea, Pearl,' Caro said getting to her feet.

'Wait a second. I've had a thought. Come on through a minute.'

The girls followed Pearl through the crowded office and beyond to the cat pens.

'I don't recognise all these cats,' Caro said, peering into cages.

'No, they're recent arrivals,' Pearl said striding ahead purposefully. She paused for a second beside one cage then reached for the catch on the adjacent one. 'Here Tootsie, good girl, here.' The cat spat with accustomed ill manners.

'What a ghastly animal!' Lucy whispered as Pearl grabbed the scraggy bundle of fur and hauled it out.

'How would you like a new home, Tootsie?' Pearl murmured chucking the animal gently under its chin. Tootsie's yellow eyes glinted.

126

Caro frowned. 'I thought you said Tootsie couldn't go to a home – that she was too wild and mean.'

'She is, but keeping her penned up here isn't doing her any good. Perhaps I was wrong about Blackheath after all. If any cat can survive without too much fussing it's Tootsie, and who knows, the experience might even soften her up a bit!'

'Can she go tonight?'

'Why not. Come on, we'll drive over. If Simon's going to be there at least I know *he'll* look after Tootsie.'

'Oh Pearl, that's brilliant!' Caro said, throwing her arms round Pearl's ample waist.

Their arrival at Blackheath caused something of a stir. Eager hands prodded and poked Tootsie who simply aimed a sharp-clawed swipe at anybody who tried to be too familiar. Simon didn't say a word but Caro could tell he was pleased to see Pearl and flattered to be put in charge of Tootsie. He was less enthralled with Lucy's offering of a folder of information about the petro-chemical industry which needed writing up.

'Mr King wants it in next week,' Lucy added, 'and if you don't make the deadline, Caro and I miss our grades as well as you so . . .'

'It's broken fingers if I mess up?' Simon said.

'You've got it, mate,' Lucy grinned. 'Listen, I've got to get home and Pearl's offered us a lift. Are you coming, Caro?'

'Yeah, just a minute,' Caro said.

'Oh sure,' Lucy said knowingly, as she left them in the deserted TV room.

Shrieks of laughter came from the upstairs landing before a blur of fur bounded into the room. Tootsie leapt onto the television and sat, insolently staring at them.

'Thanks for coming tonight,' Simon said, awkwardly picking at his sleeve.

'Will you be back at school soon?'

'As soon as I want. They're pretty easy here. It's up to me really.'

'So?'

'Tomorrow, I guess, seeing as the work's piling up for me. What was Lucy going on about . . . some shampoo?'

'Oh that! A minor triumph. But it's a start.'

'You don't give up, do you?' Simon smiled. 'Everyone's always thought I'm a lost cause, a no-hoper, except you.'

'Nobody's a lost cause,' Caro said quietly. 'Our lives have only just begun.'

'I've spent months thinking mine was a waste of time – that *everything* was, come to that. Maybe I was wrong.'

'I *know* you are,' Caro said firmly. They gazed at each other for a while until Tootsie suddenly launched herself off the television and onto Simon's shoulder. She flexed her claws painfully into Simon's shoulder before settling down. The low throaty noise might just have been a purr.

'It's a miracle!' Caro laughed, and as Simon started to chuckle she couldn't help thinking that it wasn't the only one God had worked that day.